The Write Kind of Love Story

HUSSAIN JETHAJIWALA

Published by InkQuills Publishing House
www.inkquills.in

First Edition 2024
All Rights Reserved. Copyright © 2024
ISBN: 978-81-979961-2-2

Contents

1 - Prologue

The room was dimly lighted, shadows gently moving across the walls as if they didn't want to disturb her. The air conditioner kept the room at a comfortable 24 degrees, and her laptop screen glowed with a soft blue and white light. Slow, soothing music played from the speakers, filling the space with a calming rhythm. A perfect setting to write, as Aliza may describe.

The library where fan letters piled high, overflowing with praise for her latest works. Interviews and book signings filled her calendar, a stark contrast to the quiet obscurity of her pre-fame days. Her last two novels had taken the literary world by storm, becoming instant bestsellers and catapulting her to superstardom.

Aliza sat at her desk fingers hovering over the keyboard, staring at a blank document. The blinking cursor seemed to mock her, marking each passing second. Her last two novels had been huge successes, bestsellers that made her a literary star. Now, the weight of expectations pressed heavily on her, growing with each day. No one could expect that a writer was struggling to write but only a writer knows how it feels to struggle with the darkness and loneliness to create a world of fiction.

The publisher's emails were becoming more urgent, shifting from encouragement to thinly veiled demands, each one a reminder of the looming deadline. She could almost hear their voices in her head, pushing her to create another hit, to capture magic once again. Luckily the publisher (the owner of the publishing house) was Aliza's friend. She did share her feelings with him.

"I just can't write, Fahad. It's getting difficult for me every time I sit in front of the laptop screen." Aliza said over a phone call.

"Why don't you write on paper, then?" Fahad mocked. He was eating a burger in the famous Erin's Burger café and Aliza could hear him chewing clearly and could feel the irritating chewing sound.

"Don't make this look funny. It's irritating and I can't work with your deadlines hovering over my head." She knew she could throw her tantrums over Fahad and he would not react as all to it.

"Your last two books are selling like hot burgers so don't worry about anything. Take your time. I am making good money out of it; your royalty will also keep your bank account warm. Now if you may allow, can I eat my burger at peace?"

She tapped her foot nervously, matching the beat of the music. Restlessness gnawed at her, an itch she couldn't scratch, a frustration building like a storm. Ideas swirled in her mind but never settled long enough to take shape. Her thoughts were a tangled mess, with no clear way out.

"She was struggling…." She wrote on the word document and then pressed 'backspace' to erase it completely.

With a sigh, Aliza slumped back in her chair, feeling the struggle more acutely than ever. The perfect setting she had created for inspiration now felt like a prison. The dim lights, the soothing music, the cool air—they all seemed to conspire against her. She closed her eyes, letting the frustration wash over her, feeling almost defeated by the blank screen before her.

For a moment, she allowed herself to give in to the exhaustion and pressure that had been building for weeks. She sank deeper into her chair, the fight draining out of her. The room seemed to close in around her, the shadows growing longer and darker, as if mocking her inability to write.

But just as she was about to give up, a flicker of determination sparked within her. She opened her eyes and took a deep breath, feeling a surge of resolve. The battle was far from over. She would find a way to break through the barrier, to let the words flow once more. Aliza straightened in her chair, fingers returning to the keyboard, ready to face the challenge head-on.

The cursor blinked, and she began to type.

In a world where beauty is often defined by the standards of others, she stood out like a beacon of light. Her beauty was not just skin deep; it radiated from within, illuminating everything around her.

Her eyes were like pools of liquid amber, reflecting the warmth and kindness in her heart. They sparkled with a hidden depth, hinting at a world of dreams and aspirations.

Her smile was like a ray of sunshine, infectious and heartwarming. It could brighten even the darkest of days, bringing joy to all who crossed her path. But it was not just her physical features that made her beautiful. It was her spirit, her resilience, her ability to see the good in everything and everyone.

She was a rare gem in a world obsessed with superficial beauty, a reminder that true beauty lies in the purity of the soul. And in her presence, everyone couldn't help but feel a little more beautiful themselves.

When she looked at herself in the mirror, she didn't see the beauty that others saw. Instead, she saw flaws and imperfections, each one a reminder of her own insecurities.

Her eyes lingered on the freckles that dotted her cheeks, the slight asymmetry of her features, the way her hair fell in unruly waves around her face. She sighed, wishing she could see herself through the eyes of those who saw her beauty.

But then, something shifted within her. A quiet voice whispered in her mind, reminding her of her own words. True beauty lies in the purity of the soul. She straightened her shoulders and looked at herself again, this time with a different perspective.

She saw the kindness in her eyes, the warmth in her smile, the strength in her gaze. She saw the laughter lines that crinkled around her eyes, proof of a life well-lived. She saw a woman who was imperfectly perfect, beautifully flawed.

And in that moment, she smiled at her reflection, embracing every part of herself. For she knew that true beauty was not about meeting society's standards, but about being comfortable in her own skin. And in that acceptance, she found a beauty that was truly radiant.

She was….'

Aliza suddenly stopped writing. What was she writing about? The character that she just wrote about was her own, but she had nothing to say about herself. What should she write? What is there that she could talk about herself?

Aliza sat back, her fingers hovering over the keyboard once again. She had poured her heart into describing the beauty of a fictional character, but when it came to writing about herself, she felt a blankness that was both unsettling and revealing.

She thought about the words she had written, about true beauty lying in the purity of the soul. Could she see that in herself? Could she find the beauty in her own story?

She began to type, slowly at first, the words hesitant yet honest.

I am a woman who has lived a life filled with ups and downs, triumphs and failures. I have loved and lost, laughed and cried. I have made mistakes and learned from them.

I am not perfect, far from it. I have flaws and insecurities, moments of doubt and fear. But I am also strong and resilient, capable of facing whatever life throws at me.

I am a writer, and a creator of worlds and characters. I find solace in words, in the stories that weave themselves in my mind. Writing is not just what I do; it is a part of who I am.

I am a friend, a daughter, a sister…. A sister!

Wait! Oh No! A SISTER!'

Aliza suddenly remembered about her life outside the room in which she was sitting. It was 12 in the noon and she had to go to pick her brother from Dance classes that he was having at the school and she was already half an hour late.

Aliza ran out of the room, grabbed her keys, and rushed to her car. She took the shortcut she always used to get to her brother's school, hoping to make up for lost time. But as she turned the corner, she was met with a sea of cars, all inching along at a snail's pace.

So much traffic! Why are they all taking the shortcut? I think the long cut was free of traffic and all are diverted to this shorter one making this a longer one now. Why everyone thinks the same? Are they all going to fetch their brothers and sisters from school? Are they all getting late? Why am I thinking all this? Why aren't I just honking, like others?

As she sat in traffic, Aliza couldn't help but chuckle at the absurdity of the situation. It was as if the entire city was on the road and Aliza couldn't do anything other than just honk waiting for one of the cars to open their wing and start to fly to clear the road for others.

Finally, after what felt like an eternity, Aliza arrived at the school. She parked her car and hurried to the entrance, scanning the crowd for her brother. And there he was, sitting on a bench outside the school, happily licking a candy.

She couldn't help but laugh at the sight. Her brother, with his chubby cheeks and mischievous grin, looked like a kid in a candy store. She walked over to him, ruffling his hair affectionately.

"Hey, little troublemaker. Ready to go home?" she asked, smiling.

"Yep!" he replied, jumping up from the bench. "But can we stop for ice cream on the way?"

Aliza laughed, nodding. "Of course, anything for my favourite dance star."

As they walked back to the car, Nadeem couldn't contain his excitement about the impending ice cream stop. "I can already taste the chocolate swirl," he said, rubbing his hands together eagerly.

Aliza chuckled. "You know, Nadeem, most kids don't need dance classes to get ice cream. They just ask nicely."

Nadeem contended. "Well, I like to do things the hard way. Keeps life interesting." The reply he gave may appear like coming from a mature person, but he was only 15 years old. The philosophy that this kid could talk about was just phenomenal at his age.

They got into the car, and as they drove, Nadeem started humming a tune.

"You seem pretty happy for someone who supposedly doesn't like dancing," Aliza remarked, raising an eyebrow.

Nadeem shrugged. "Who said anything about liking it? I just go for the snacks they have afterwards."

Aliza laughed. "Well, whatever works for you, buddy. Just don't eat too much ice cream, or you might not fit through the door."

Nadeem pretended to gasp in shock. "Are you saying I'm fat?"

Nadeem said while keeping one hand on his stomach and other with rolled fist on his temple.

Aliza feigned innocence. "Of course not, Nadeem. I'm just saying, we wouldn't want you to get stuck in the car door. The car is costly and we won't like to damage it further."

They both burst out laughing, enjoying the light-hearted banter. As they pulled into the ice cream shop, Aliza couldn't help but feel grateful for moments like these, when she could forget about deadlines and expectations and just enjoy being with her brother.

As they sat in the ice cream shop, enjoying their treats, Aliza's thoughts drifted to their childhood. It had been tough after their parents passed away in a car accident around 12 years ago, but they had always had each other. She remembered how Nadeem had struggled to fit in with their maternal uncle's family, always feeling like an outsider.

"I'm glad we have moments like this, Nadeem," Aliza said, breaking the silence. "It's important to cherish the good times."

Nadeem nodded; his expression serious for a moment. "Yeah, I never felt like I belonged there, you know? It's different with you. 'There'… I mean you know."

Aliza reached across the table and squeezed his hand. "I know, Nadeem. And I'm glad you're here with me. Let's hope that the books keep on selling till you reach 18 years of age and after that I'll kick you out of the house and live all alone with my royalty and enjoy the rest of my life."

"You can't do that. I may need to stay with you till I find some rich girl to marry. That would take at least 10 more years from now." Nadeem and Aliza laughed again.

They finished their ice cream and then moved out after having a great time.

"Hey, how about we have a movie night tonight? Just the two of us, like old times," she suggested.

Nadeem's face lit up. "That sounds awesome! Can we watch that new action movie you were talking about?"

"Absolutely," Aliza replied, smiling. "It's a plan then. Let's head home and get comfortable."

As they drove back, Aliza couldn't help but feel grateful for the bond she shared with her brother. Despite the challenges they had faced, they had always been there for each other. And in moments like these, she knew that their parents were watching over them, proud of the strong, loving siblings they had become.

2 - The Chaos

Later that night, after an evening filled with laughter and a movie, Aliza found herself lying in bed, staring at the ceiling. The room was quiet, save for the faint hum of the air conditioner. Nadeem was fast asleep in his room, and the house felt unusually still.

As she lay there, memories from the past began to flood her mind, dragging her back to that fateful day twelve years ago.

*****

She was only fourteen, and Nadeem was just three. They were returning home from a family outing, a rare and joyous occasion. Their parents had taken them to the beach, and the day had been filled with laughter, sandcastles, and ice cream. As they drove back, the sun was setting, casting a golden glow over the landscape.

Aliza was dozing off in the back seat, Nadeem asleep beside her, clutching his favorite stuffed toy. She remembered the soft hum of the car engine, the soothing rhythm that always lulled her into sleep. Her parents' voices drifted in and out of her consciousness, their gentle conversation a comforting background noise.

But then, everything changed in an instant.

A loud horn blared; jolting Aliza awake. She barely had time to register what was happening before a violent jolt threw her against the side of the car. The sound of screeching tires and shattering glass filled the air. The world spun around her, and then everything went black.

When Aliza regained consciousness, the first thing she felt was pain. It radiated through her body, but the most intense pain came from her heart as she realized the gravity of the situation. The car was on its side, the windows shattered. She could hear

Nadeem crying, his small voice filled with fear.

"Mom? Dad?" she called out, her voice trembling. But there was no response.

With all the strength she could muster, Aliza crawled towards Nadeem, her body aching with every movement. She saw her parents slumped over in the front seats, motionless. Panic surged through her, but she knew she had to stay calm for Nadeem.

"It's okay, Nadeem," she whispered, trying to soothe him as she unbuckled his seatbelt and pulled him close. "I'm here. I'm right here."

She managed to find her phone and call for help, her hands shaking so badly she could barely dial the number. The wait for the emergency responders felt like an eternity. She held Nadeem tightly, whispering words of comfort even as tears streamed down her face.

*****

Aliza blinked, the memories fading back into the depths of her mind. She felt the familiar sting of tears but took a deep breath, pushing the pain aside. She turned on her side, curling up under the covers, and closed her eyes.

In the quiet darkness, she reminded herself that she and Nadeem had survived. They had each other, and that bond had helped them through the toughest times. She knew their parents would want them to be happy and to cherish the good moments.

As sleep finally began to claim her, Aliza made a silent promise to herself. She would keep fighting, both for her own sake and for Nadeem's. No matter how tough things got, she would find a way to keep moving forward, just as she always had.

And with that thought, she drifted off into a peaceful sleep, the memories of the past blending with dreams of a hopeful future.

*****

The next morning, Aliza woke up with a sense of dread. She had a meeting scheduled at her publisher's office to discuss the plan for her next book.

She looked at the clock next to her bed and knew that she is already a lot late.

"Nadeem, wake up! We're both late!" She jumped out of bed, her heart racing.

Nadeem groaned, barely opening his eyes. "Just five more minutes, Aliza…"

"No time for that!" Aliza grabbed a pillow and playfully whacked him with it. "We're seriously late, Nadeem!"

Nadeem sat up, rubbing his eyes. "Alright, alright. I'm up. What's the rush?"

"I have that meeting with Fahad and the marketing team, remember? And you have your school presentation that you have almost forget, remember anything?"

Nadeem's eyes widened as he realized the urgency. "Oh no, I completely forgot! Quick, get ready. I'll handle breakfast."

Aliza rushed to the bathroom, quickly brushing her teeth and washing her face. She threw on a simple yet professional outfit, barely taking the time to check her reflection in the mirror. Nadeem, meanwhile, scrambled to make some toast and coffee, trying to multi-task without much success.

As Aliza emerged from the bedroom, Nadeem handed her a piece of toast. "Here, it's not much, but it'll have to do."

"Thanks, Nadeem. You're a lifesaver." Aliza grabbed the toast and her bag, heading for the door. "Don't forget your notes for the presentation!"

"Got it!" Nadeem called back, shoving papers into his backpack.

They both rushed out of the apartment, practically running to their respective destinations. Aliza hailed a cab, her mind racing with thoughts about the upcoming meeting. She munched on the toast, trying to calm her nerves.

As Aliza prepared for the day, she couldn't shake off the feeling of frustration and anxiety gnawing at her. She had nothing for the new book, and the pressure was mounting. She hurriedly gathered her things, still trying to wrap her mind around the meeting that awaited her.

In the car, her thoughts raced even faster than the traffic. She gripped the steering wheel tightly, her mind conjuring up potential excuses for her lack of progress.

"Maybe I could tell them I'm still doing research," she thought, wincing at how flimsy that sounded. "Or that I've been exploring new themes but need more time to develop them... No, that won't cut it either. They'll see right through it."

She sighed, her frustration bubbling over. "I could say I need a break to recharge my creative batteries. But what if they think I'm just slacking off?"

Aliza turned onto the main road, the familiar route doing little to calm her nerves. "What if I just tell them the truth? That I'm completely stuck and don't know how to move forward. But then what? Will they lose faith in me?"

The car ahead of her braked suddenly, jolting her back to reality. She slammed on the brakes, narrowly avoiding a collision. Her heart raced, both from the near-miss and the weight of her thoughts.

"Get it together, Aliza," she muttered to herself. "You can't fall apart now."

She took a deep breath, trying to steady her nerves. "Maybe I should just ask for more time. Fahad's a friend, he'll understand… but how much time can I really ask for?"

As she drove, her mind kept spinning in circles, rehearsing various explanations and excuses. None of them felt right. None of them felt good enough.

She passed a coffee shop and considered stopping for a caffeine boost but decided against it. She was already running late, and the last thing she needed was to show up even later.

"What if I pitch a few vague ideas and see if they latch onto any of them?" she wondered. "Maybe that'll buy me some time to come up with something solid."

The thought brought a tiny flicker of hope, but it was quickly extinguished by doubt. "No, they'll want specifics. They'll want a clear direction."

She arrived at the publishing house parking lot and turned off the engine. Sitting in the silence, she could feel her heartbeat in her throat. "I need to pull myself together. I've faced worse situations before. I just need to get through this meeting."

She glanced in the rearview mirror, giving herself a stern look. "You've got this, Aliza. Just be honest and do your best."

With a final deep breath, she grabbed her bag and stepped out of the car, ready to face whatever awaited her inside.

*****

Aliza arrived at the publishing house a few minutes early, hoping to gather her thoughts. The sleek, modern building loomed before her, its glass facade reflecting the bustling city around it. She took a deep breath and walked inside, determined to face the music.

The interior was a blend of old-world charm and contemporary design. The walls were adorned with framed book covers and vintage photographs, showcasing the rich history of the publishing house. A large, antique publishing machine stood proudly in the center of the hall, a symbol of the legacy that Fahad's grandfather had built.

The machine was nearly a century old, its metal parts gleaming under the soft glow of the lights. It was a reminder of a bygone era, when printing books was a laborious and meticulous process. Fahad often spoke fondly of his grandfather's work with Gandhi Ji and other revolutionaries, and the machine was a tangible link to that history.

In the conference room, Fahad, her publisher, was already there, along with the marketing team. They greeted her warmly, but Aliza could sense the anticipation in the air. She sat down, trying to muster a confident smile.

"Good morning, Aliza!" Fahad said, clapping his hands together. "How are you doing today?"

"Morning, Fahad. I'm... managing," Aliza replied, her voice not quite as enthusiastic as she had hoped. She took her seat and took a deep breath.

"Great, great," Fahad said, oblivious to her lack of excitement.

"We have a lot to discuss. The last two books were phenomenal hits, and we want to keep that momentum going. So, let's talk about your next masterpiece." Fahad although knew the state of mind of Aliza but he couldn't show it in the conference room because after all he had to keep things working and for that sometimes he needs to keep relationships aside.

Aliza nodded, feeling a lump form in her throat. The marketing team, consisting of three people, shuffled some papers and looked at her expectantly.

"Before we dive in," Fahad continued, "I just want to remind everyone how crucial this next book is. We're talking about expanding your reach, international book tours, potential movie deals—"

"Movie deals?" Aliza interjected; eyebrows raised. "We haven't even started the book yet, Fahad."

"Details, details," Fahad said with a dismissive wave. "We're just thinking ahead, you know? Planning for the future. We want to make your name stand out among the top international writers and for that we need something special from you."

"Right," Aliza muttered, feeling her frustration rise.

The head of marketing, Ragini, leaned forward. She was a tall woman with sharp features and an even sharper mind. "Aliza, we've been brainstorming some ideas for themes and genres that are trending right now. Have you considered writing a thriller? Or maybe a dystopian novel? Those are really hot at the moment."

Aliza sighed inwardly. "I appreciate the suggestions, Ragini, but I'm really struggling with inspiration. I don't even have a basic plot, let alone a genre."

Fahad jumped in; his voice filled with faux optimism. "That's okay! Let's brainstorm together. Throw some ideas out there, and we'll help you shape them."

"Okay," Aliza said, forcing a smile. "How about a story about a writer who is under so much pressure to deliver a new book that she starts imagining her publisher as a giant monster, and her marketing team as… monster's advisory group?"

The room went silent. Then, Fahad burst into laughter, followed by the hesitant chuckles of the marketing team.

"Very funny, Aliza," Fahad said, wiping a tear from his eye. "But seriously, we need something concrete."

Aliza leaned back in her chair, rubbing her temples. "I know, I know. It's just… I've hit a wall. The ideas aren't coming like they used to."

Ragini tapped her pen on the table thoughtfully. "Maybe you need a change of scenery? Sometimes a new environment can spark creativity."

Aliza shook her head. "I've tried that. Coffee shops, parks, even a cabin in the woods. Nothing's working."

Another member of the marketing team, Dave, chimed in. "What if you drew inspiration from your own life? Readers love authenticity."

Aliza snorted. "What, like a memoir? 'How to Write a Bestseller While Losing Your Sanity'? No offense, but my life isn't exactly page-turner material. And also, I have already talked about everything about my life in the first two books, so definitely nothing left there to explore."

Fahad leaned forward; his expression serious for the first time.

"Aliza, we all know you're capable of greatness. You've done it before, and you can do it again. What's really holding you back?"

Aliza hesitated, then took a deep breath. "Honestly, Fahad, it's the pressure. The expectations. I'm terrified of disappointing everyone."

The room fell silent again, this time with a more sympathetic tone. Ragini nodded understandingly. "We get that, Aliza. And we're here to support you, not add to your stress. Maybe we need to rethink our approach."

Dave perked up. "How about we organize a writing retreat? Just a few days away with no distractions, no deadlines. Just you and your creativity."

Aliza considered it. "That... actually sounds nice. But I can't just abandon everything. I have responsibilities."

Fahad smiled. "Leave that to us. We'll handle your commitments here. You just focus on finding your inspiration. And I'll talk to Nadeem's school, they love me. I can arrange few days holiday for him for sure."

Aliza felt a flicker of hope. "Alright, let's give it a shot. But no promises, okay?"

"Of course," Fahad said, grinning. "Now, let's talk logistics. Where would you like to go?"

As they brainstormed potential retreat locations, Aliza felt a weight lift off her shoulders. Maybe this retreat could be the key to unlocking her creativity again.

*****

Aliza and Fahad were now in Fahad's office, a cozy space filled with books and papers. Fahad was lounging back in his chair, happily munching on a burger and looking completely relaxed. Aliza couldn't help but laugh at the sight.

"You know, Fahad, you're a completely different person here. So serious and professional," she said, shaking her head.

Fahad chuckled, wiping his hands on a napkin. "Well, what can I say? Gotta keep up appearances in front of the team. Can't let them see the real me, can I? Will they respect me then? They'll start ignoring my calls just like you. I can't afford that. I pay them money to work for me, well the same goes to you but still you are different, you are my friend."

"And what is the real you like?" Aliza teased, raising an eyebrow.

Fahad leaned back, a playful glint in his eyes. "Oh, just a carefree guy who loves his burgers and couldn't care less about work," he joked.

Aliza laughed, shaking her head. "You're lucky I know the real you then."

Fahad giggled. "Indeed, you are. So, about your retreat. Have you thought about any location where you can get the inspiration that you are looking for? Anything that you were thinking?"

Aliza thought a bit but got nothing in her system. She was as blank as she always been thinking about this new book. When Aliza said nothing, Fahad came forward.

"What about Varanasi?"

"Varanasi? That's an interesting choice. Why Varanasi?" Aliza asked, intrigued.

Fahad leaned forward, his eyes sparkling with enthusiasm.

"Varanasi is a city unlike any other. It's steeped in history, culture, and spirituality. The ghats, the temples, the narrow lanes bustling with life—it's a sensory overload that can really ignite your senses and spark your creativity."

Aliza nodded thoughtfully. "That does sound intriguing. The spiritual energy of the place could be just what I need to find my inspiration. Also, this will make our new book easy to be picked up by the people who really want to explore the Indian realm."

Fahad smiled. "Exactly! And let's not forget the incredible food. The street food in Varanasi is legendary. Who knows, maybe a taste of some local delicacies will awaken your muse."

Aliza chuckled. "Food for thought, quite literally."

Fahad's grin widened. "And the people! Varanasi is a melting pot of cultures and traditions. Interacting with the locals, hearing their stories, experiencing their way of life—it could provide a whole new perspective for your book."

Aliza's eyes lit up with excitement. "You know, I think you might be onto something with Varanasi. It could be just the change of scenery I need to break out of this rut."

Fahad leaned forward with a new thought, "Have you ever been to Assi Ghat? It's a place where you can see the full circle of life. From birth to death, it's all there. It's a place that truly makes you appreciate the beauty and fragility of life."

Fahad continued, "First you see the enjoyment at Assi Ghat, the subah-e-Banaras and the rides and all the joyful things around and then watching the end of life at Manikarnika Ghat. As if you have seen the full circle of life in a single evening. It's a reminder of our mortality, but also a celebration of life. It's a place that will make you reflect, inspire you, and maybe even spark some new ideas for your book."

Aliza thought for a moment, then smiled. "Alright, let's do it. Let's go to Varanasi."

Fahad grinned. "Great! I'll make all the arrangements. It's going to be an unforgettable experience, I promise."

As they continued to plan their trip, Aliza felt a sense of excitement building within her. Maybe this retreat was exactly what she needed to break free from her creative block and find inspiration once again.

After finalizing their plans, Fahad picked up the phone and called Nadeem's school. "Hello, this is Fahad from HJ Publishing House. I'm calling to request leave for Nadeem for a few days. We're going on a family trip."

The school secretary recognized Fahad's name. "Oh, Mr. Fahad! Of course, Nadeem can have the leave. We appreciate all the books your publishing house supplies to our school. Have a great trip!"

Fahad thanked the secretary and hung up with a smile. "All set. Nadeem's school is happy to grant him leave."

Aliza and Nadeem headed home to pack for their trip. Aliza gathered her essentials, including her laptop and a notebook for jotting down any ideas that might come to her during the trip. Nadeem, on the other hand, was busy deciding which toys and books to bring along.

As they packed, Aliza's mind was buzzing with anticipation. She couldn't wait to explore Varanasi and immerse herself in its rich culture and history. She hoped that the trip would not only help her find inspiration for her new book but also create lasting memories with Nadeem.

Once they were all packed and ready to go, they set off for the airport.

*****

As the flight got airborne, a sudden excitement took over Aliza. She felt a thrill she hadn't experienced in a long time, her heart racing with anticipation. She took out her notebook and began to write a few sentences. They were vague, disjointed thoughts, but the act of writing them down felt liberating. It was as if a dam had burst, and the words, no matter how unclear, started to flow.

Nadeem, sitting by the window, was equally excited. His face was pressed against the glass, eyes wide with wonder as he looked at the city shrinking below them. "Sissy, look! The buildings look like tiny toys!" he exclaimed; his voice filled with awe.

Aliza smiled, sharing his excitement. "They do, don't they? It's amazing how different everything looks from up here."

On the aisle seat next to Aliza was a man who caught her attention. He looked like a total hippie, with a long beard and a bun on his head. His attire was a curious mix of a saint and a beachgoer, with loose, colorful clothes and beaded necklaces. He exuded a carefree aura that was hard to ignore.

The man turned to Aliza with a curious smile. "Are you a writer?" he asked, his voice mellow and soothing. "Going to Varanasi for your muse?"

Aliza felt amused that how he figured out but didn't ask anything and simply nodded, not wanting to get too engaged in conversation. She was still processing her own thoughts and feelings about the journey ahead.

The man didn't seem to mind her silence. Instead, he leaned back in his seat and started to share his thoughts, almost as if he were talking to himself. "You know, Varanasi is a magical place. They say it's the city where the circle of life is most visible. Birth, death, and everything in between. It's all right there, in front of you. Quite a place for inspiration, don't you think? And also, this is the oldest city of the world, I don't claim it but many does."

Aliza offered a polite smile but kept her focus on her notebook, scribbling down more thoughts. Despite her reluctance to engage, she couldn't help but find his words intriguing. There was a certain charm in his nonchalant philosophy.

The man continued, his tone becoming more animated. "I remember my first trip to Varanasi. I was like you, searching for something, though I didn't know what it was at the time. But the city has a way of showing you things, you know? Sometimes in the most unexpected ways."

Aliza glanced at him, still not saying much, but she nodded to show she was listening. He chuckled, sensing her apprehension. "Don't worry, I won't bore you with my life's story. Just enjoy the journey. It's just the beginning, after all. And you never know what you'll discover in your journey. I know you'll not return with blank papers from there." He smiled and Aliza couldn't understand why but those words were deep for her. She thought of writing them in the notebook and she did.

She couldn't help but smile at his cheerful demeanor. It was hard to stay aloof when someone was so unabashedly positive. Aliza looked out the window, where Nadeem was still glued to the view. The sky stretched out endlessly, a reminder of how vast and full of possibilities the world was.

The man turned back to his own musings, and Aliza returned to her notebook, jotting down snippets of thoughts and ideas. The sentences were still vague, but they carried a sense of hope and excitement. The flight continued smoothly, and with each passing minute, her anticipation grew. And finally, she was in the city of Varanasi.

3 - Varanasi – Where Miracles Happen!

Finally, Aliza and Nadeem reached Varanasi. As always, the airport was far from the main city, and it felt like traveling through a maze where the roads seemed to narrow with each turn. After about two hours, they finally arrived at Aliza's hotel, which was conveniently close to one of Varanasi's main attractions, Assi Ghat.

As they approached, the bustling atmosphere immediately struck Aliza. Assi Ghat was teeming with life—locals and tourists alike crowded the steps leading down to the Ganges River. This ghat, one of the oldest and most significant in Varanasi, was a hub of activity from dawn until dusk. People came to perform rituals, bathe in the sacred waters, and witness the mesmerizing Ganga River Light Ceremony in the evening.

The ghat's historical and spiritual significance added to its charm. The confluence of the Assi and Ganges rivers was considered particularly auspicious. The hustle bustle of the crowd filled the air, creating an ambiance that was both chaotic and serene.

Aliza and Nadeem rushed to their room, excitement bubbling over. The first thing they did was jump on the bed like children, laughing and bouncing on the soft mattress. It was a moment of pure, carefree joy that they both savored.

"I can't remember the last time I did this," Aliza giggled, sinking into the plush pillows.

"Me neither," Nadeem agreed, grinning from ear to ear. "It feels good to let loose."

After their playful antics, they took turns freshening up in the bathroom. Aliza went first, enjoying the warm water that washed away the fatigue of their journey. She emerged feeling refreshed and rejuvenated, wrapping herself in a cozy robe.

Nadeem was next, and he took his time. He discovered the luxurious bathtub and couldn't resist sinking into it. The hot water and fragrant bubbles were irresistible, and he closed his eyes, savoring the moment.

"This is heaven," he murmured to himself, losing track of time.

Meanwhile, Aliza unpacked their bags and arranged a few things. She was just about to call Nadeem to hurry up when the phone rang. It was the receptionist.

"Hello, Ms. Aliza," the receptionist said warmly. "I just wanted to inform you that the Ganga Ceremony is about to begin at the ghat. You really shouldn't miss it."

"Oh, thank you for the reminder!" Aliza exclaimed. "We'll be there shortly."

She hung up and called out to Nadeem. "Nadeem, hurry up! The Ganga Ceremony is about to start, and we don't want to miss it."

Nadeem reluctantly climbed out of the tub, wrapping himself in a towel. "Alright, alright. Coming in a bit." He came out and dressed himself like an obedient child and then came out of the hotel room with his sister. The moment they stepped out of their hotel, Aliza and Nadeem were greeted by a sea of people heading towards Assi Ghat. The crowd was so dense that only a multitude of heads bobbing up and down was visible, creating an almost surreal wave of humanity. It was as if the entire city had converged upon this sacred spot, drawn by an invisible magnetic pull.

Despite the crowd, a palpable sense of excitement filled the air. Aliza and Nadeem joined the throng, moving with the tide of pilgrims and visitors. The cacophony of voices, the scent of incense, and the vibrant energy around them were both overwhelming and exhilarating.

As they walked, the mighty Ganges remained hidden from view, obscured by the sheer number of people. The river, which they had come so far to see, seemed to be playing a game of hide and seek. With each step, the anticipation grew. The walk, though only about 50 meters, felt like a journey through a living tapestry of devotion and tradition.

Finally, they caught sight of the platform leading towards the ghat. The scene that unfolded before them was nothing short of majestic. The entire area was bathed in a warm, golden glow from the yellow lighting, casting a magical hue over everything. The preparations for the Ganga River Light Ceremony were in full swing, and the sight was breathtaking.

Priests dressed in traditional attire moved gracefully, setting up the ornate oil lamps and other ritualistic paraphernalia. The air was thick with the scent of flowers and the sound of people, creating an atmosphere that was both festive and reverent. The platform itself seemed to glow, a beacon of spiritual energy and cultural richness.

"It's beautiful," Aliza whispered, her eyes wide with wonder.

Nadeem nodded, equally captivated. "It's like a scene from a dream. The photos we've seen don't do it justice." Nadeem was busy in clicking every nook and corner of the ghats and was wondering how he could get more of the scenic beauty that he was witnessing.

As they moved closer, they could finally see the Ganges. The river, now illuminated by the golden lights, appeared almost ethereal. The reflections of the lights danced on the water, creating a mesmerizing, shimmering effect. It was as if the Ganges itself was participating in the ceremony, its waters glistening with divine light.

They found a spot among the crowd, allowing them a perfect

view of the Ceremony preparations. The anticipation in the air was almost tangible as more people gathered, waiting for the ceremony to begin. Aliza felt a sense of unity and shared purpose among the crowd. Everyone was here for the same reason—to witness the Ganga River Light Ceremony, a timeless tradition that connected the past with the present.

As the first lights began to start of a hush fell over the crowd. The rhythmic sound of the music and the sight of the light bearers moving in unison with the large, flaming lamps created an almost hypnotic effect. Aliza felt her heart swell with emotion. The beauty of the ceremony and the devotion of the people around her combined to create a moment of pure, transcendent awe.

"This is incredible," Nadeem said softly, his voice filled with reverence. "I can see why they say you have to experience it to understand it."

"Yes," Aliza agreed, her eyes never leaving the scene before her. "This is something we'll remember forever. And the energy of this place is something that really can't be explained in words."

Nadeem replied almost instantly, "I always knew you were a bad writer. You always fell short of words." He smiled.

"Shut up." They both smiled and fell silent for a while and presented all their attention to the ceremony that was happening in front of them. The chanting was surreal.

They stood there, side by side, soaking in the beauty and spirituality of the Ganga Ceremony. In that moment, surrounded by the ancient city of Varanasi and its timeless rituals, they felt deeply connected to something greater than themselves.

"It's beautiful, isn't it?" Nadeem said, standing beside her. His voice broke her reverie, but she nodded in agreement.

"It's overwhelming," she admitted, "but in a good way."

"Mesmerizing," Aliza whispered, her eyes fixed on the glowing lights and rhythmic movements of the priests. Suddenly, she heard a laugh behind her. Startled, she turned around to see a man standing there. He had an air of confidence and ease about him that set him apart from the crowd.

The man looked like a foreigner but was unmistakably Indian. His pitch-black hair flowed freely around his shoulders, and he wore loose, comfortable clothing that seemed both practical and stylish. His skin was much fairer compared to those around him, and his beard was impeccable, giving him a refined yet rugged appearance. There was no denying he was strikingly handsome, but the way he had laughed at her comment made Aliza's cheeks flush with anger.

What's so funny?" Aliza snapped, her irritation bubbling to the surface.

The man raised his hands in a gesture of apology, his smile still lingering. "I'm sorry," he said, his voice smooth and calming. "I didn't mean to offend you. It's just that your reaction to the Ceremony was so... well, picture-perfect, like something out of a book. We don't usually talk like that anymore, do we?"

Aliza's irritation flared again, but curiosity won over. "What do you mean?" she asked, trying to keep her voice steady. She really wanted to understand what he was getting at.

The man hesitated, searching for the right words. "I mean... how should I put this? It's like how rich people talk, you know? 'Oh wow, this is so good,' 'Mmmm, wow,' and all that," he said, mimicking an exaggeratedly posh accent. He laughed softly, clearly amused by his own imitation. "It's just that people who usually stay in their comfort zones get startled by everything they come across when they step out."

Aliza bristled at his words. "I really didn't want to offend you," the man added quickly, seeing her reaction. "But it's the first time I've seen someone react like this to the Ganga Ceremony."

"I think you should learn to appreciate things," Aliza retorted sharply, "and most importantly, mind your own business." Without waiting for a response, she grabbed Nadeem's hand and pulled him away, moving to the other side of the crowd to distance themselves from the man.

As they walked away, Aliza felt a mixture of anger and embarrassment. "Who does he think he is?" she muttered, more to herself than to Nadeem. "Judging people like that."

Nadeem squeezed her hand reassuringly. "Don't let it get to you, Aliza. Some people just don't know how to interact without being condescending."

They found a new spot, still with a good view of the Ceremony. Aliza took a deep breath, trying to let go of the encounter. The ceremony was in full swing now, with the public moving in synchrony, the flames of their lamps casting a golden glow on the river. The lamps filled the air, creating a mesmerizing atmosphere that drew Aliza back into the moment.

She glanced around, noticing the diverse crowd. People from all walks of life had come together to witness this ancient ritual, their faces lit with the same awe and reverence she felt. It was a humbling sight, reminding her of the shared human experience.

Nadeem leaned in closer, his voice soft. "Isn't it amazing how something so ancient can still captivate people from all over the world?"

Aliza nodded, her irritation finally melting away. "It really is. And maybe that guy had a point, in a way. We do need to step out of our comfort zones to truly appreciate things."

Nadeem smiled. "That's the spirit. Let's just focus on this beautiful moment."

They stood there, hand in hand, letting the serenity of the Ganga Ceremony wash over them. The man's comments faded into the background as they immersed themselves in the sacred ceremony, finding peace in the shared experience and the timeless beauty of Varanasi.

*****

After the Ceremony, they decided to take the boat ride. As the boat gently drifted along the sacred waters of the Ganges, Aliza and Nadeem sat in awe of the mystical beauty that surrounded them. The ghats, adorned with flickering lamps and echoing with the sounds of distant chats, looked like something out of a dream.

"These ghats are so beautiful and looking so good because of all these lightings and all," Aliza whispered, her voice barely audible over the gentle lapping of the water against the boat.

Nadeem nodded in agreement; his eyes wide with wonder. "It's like we've stepped into another world," he replied, his voice filled with reverence. He was continuously taking photos of everything.

They sat in silence for a while, simply taking in the breathtaking sights around them. The soft glow of the surrounding lights danced on the water, creating a mesmerizing reflection that seemed to stretch on for eternity.

As they approached Manikarnika Ghat, the atmosphere shifted. The air grew heavy with a sense of solemnity, and the boat owner's words resonated deeply with them.

The boat owner told Nadeen not to take any photo of this place where the cremation was happening. "We must respect this place," the old man said quietly, as if afraid to disturb the peacefulness of the moment. "These are sacred grounds, and we should honor the souls that rest here." The boat owner too took a long breath whole crossing this particular ghat. Aliza saw the expressions of the boat owner and thought to write about it in her book. It was something that should be written for sure. The muse that she was finding was somehow now clearly visible to her.

Aliza nodded, her heart heavy with the weight of the centuries-old tradition that surrounded them. She reached out and gently squeezed Nadeem's hand, a silent gesture of solidarity and understanding.

They continued their journey in silence, each lost in their own thoughts. The beauty of the ghats was undeniable, but it was tempered by a deep sense of respect and reverence for the souls that had passed on.

As they neared the end of their boat ride, the atmosphere lightened once more. The sounds of the city began to filter in, breaking the spell of silence that had enveloped them.

"It's time to go back," Aliza said softly, a hint of reluctance in her voice.

Nadeem nodded, his gaze lingering on the ghats for a moment longer. "Yes, but we'll come back tomorrow," he replied, determination shining in his eyes. "There's still so much more to see and experience."

With one last glance at the ghats, they turned and made their way back to the shore, their hearts full of the beauty and mystery of Varanasi.

The ride was filled with joy and a sense of inner peace. The illuminated boats added to the enchanting atmosphere, blending beautifully with the dark night.

As Aliza and Nadeem approached their hotel, they noticed the familiar figure of the man sitting in the hallway. Aliza's irritation flared up again, and she marched over to him, her steps purposeful.

"Excuse me," she said, her voice sharp. "Are you following us?"

The man looked up, a faint smile playing on his lips. "No, not at all," he replied calmly. "I'm actually staying at this hotel."

Aliza folded her arms, unconvinced. "Really? What a coincidence," she said, skepticism evident in her tone.

Nadeem, sensing the tension, stepped in. "It's possible, Aliza. Varanasi is a popular destination, after all," he said, trying to diffuse the situation. "We should not create a scene here. Let's go."

The man nodded, his smile widening slightly. "Exactly. And this hotel is known for its excellent service and convenient location," he added, gesturing around the lobby. He had a sheepish smile over his face and Aliza didn't like that at all.

After Aliza and Nadeem headed to their room, Aliza remained upset, her mind still replaying the encounter with the man. She didn't engage much with Nadeem, lost in her thoughts as she entered their room and sat on the bed, staring out of the window at the twinkling lights of Varanasi.

Meanwhile, the man, waited patiently for them to disappear into their room before heading towards the receptionist. The receptionist, a young woman with a warm smile, greeted him politely.

"Hello sir, how can we help you?" she asked, her voice friendly.

"Well, I want to check in," the man replied, returning her smile.

"Certainly, can I have your name, sir?"

"This is Ahaan," he said, handing over his identification. "Let me do the entry for you in the register," he added, reaching out for the register with a polite gesture.

The receptionist, happy to oblige, handed him the register. As Ahaan filled in his details, his eyes scanned the page, looking for the names of the other guests. Finally, he found what he was looking for—Aliza and Nadeem.

Ahaan smiled to himself, a plan forming in his mind. He had been following Aliza and Nadeem, intrigued by their reactions and eager to join in their adventure. This unexpected turn of events only added to his excitement.

As he finished checking in, Ahaan thanked the receptionist and headed towards his room, his mind buzzing with possibilities. He couldn't wait to see what the night had in store for him and his new acquaintances, Aliza and Nadeem.

4 - The Blooming Love

The next day, Aliza and Nadeem woke up early, eager to explore the ghats in the morning light. By 6 AM, they were already making their way down to the river, the cool dawn air invigorating their senses. As they approached the ghats, the atmosphere buzzed with an energy different from the evening before.

The morning Ganga River Light Ceremony was more subdued compared to the evening one, but the serenity of the river and the gentle breeze created a peaceful ambiance. The ghats were bustling with activity, tourists were engaged in morning prayers and yoga sessions.

They walked along the ghats, observing the surroundings and soaking in the atmosphere. The early morning light cast a golden hue over everything, making the river shimmer and the ancient steps of the ghats glow with a warm, inviting light.

Various priests and nomads found their home near these ghats and were interesting enough for Nadeem to take some photos of them. Aliza saw everything from a distance. She was a kind of a girl who didn't want to involve in anything but just want to observe it from a distance.

As they continued their stroll, they came across a group of children reciting nursery rhymes. The melodies blended harmoniously with the sound of the flowing river, creating a mesmerizing symphony. They all were the students at the nearby Banaras Playgroup and were preparing for their annual fest. They had a great sense of music and were having a great time together.

"Let's sit here for a while," Nadeem suggested, pointing to a spot where they could sit and enjoy their practice.

Aliza agreed, and they found a comfortable place to settle down.

They sat side by side, letting the music and the rhythmic atmosphere wash over them. The scene was a perfect blend of tranquility and liveliness, offering them a unique glimpse into the soul of Varanasi.

After some time, Aliza noticed a group of children playing nearby, their laughter ringing out joyfully. She smiled, feeling a sense of peace and contentment. "This place is magical," she said softly. "I feel like we could stay here forever."

Nadeem squeezed her hand gently. "I know what you mean. There's something timeless about this city. It's like every moment here is a connection to the past and a celebration of the present." They sat in silence for a while longer, simply enjoying the moment. The morning sun climbed higher in the sky, gradually warming the air. The ghats, now fully bathed in sunlight, looked even more enchanting.

"We should explore some more before it gets too crowded," Nadeem suggested, standing up and offering Aliza his hand.

She took it, and they continued their walk, visiting various ghats and marveling at the sights. They watched artists creating portrait of various things on the ghats, and vendors setting up their stalls, preparing for the day's business.

As they wandered, they made a mental note of the places they wanted to revisit. The morning had been a perfect start to their day, filled with unexpected moments of beauty and serenity.

Eventually, they decided to take a break and enjoy a traditional breakfast at one of the small riverside cafes. They found a cozy spot with a perfect view of the river, where they ordered steaming cups of Tea and plates of freshly made Funnel cakes.

"This is the best breakfast I've ever had," Aliza said, savoring the flavors.

Nadeem laughed. "I think everything tastes better when you're in a place like this."

As they ate, they talked about their plans for the rest of the day, excited about the adventures that lay ahead. They were eager to delve deeper into the heart of Varanasi, to explore its narrow lanes, ancient places, and bustling markets.

Just as they were finishing their meal, Aliza glanced up and noticed Ahaan approaching their table. She felt a flicker of annoyance but quickly suppressed it, reminding herself to keep an open mind.

"Good morning," Ahaan greeted them with a friendly smile. "I hope I'm not intruding. I just wanted to say hello and apologize again for any misunderstanding last night."

Nadeem smiled warmly, but after noticing Aliza's expression, he stopped smiling. Aliza was still angry and didn't want to engage in any kind of conversation.

Although no one asked him, Ahaan sat down, with an extra-wide smile on his face. "It's nice to see familiar faces in such a vast city. How has your morning been?"

"You can see many familiar faces around if you start looking in some other direction, and definitely we had a great start to the day, but now it seems we have a problem," Aliza replied, her irritation still intact. "Now will you please excuse us? Or do you need to irritate us further?"

Ahaan kept smiling, unfazed by her harsh words. "I'm sorry if I upset you," he said calmly. "Let me properly introduce myself. My name is Ahaan."

Aliza didn't respond, her silence spoke volumes.

Ahaan continued, his smile never faltering. "I know you, Aliza. You are the writer. I am a big fan of yours."

Aliza's eyes narrowed with suspicion. "A fan, huh? And how exactly do you know about my writing?"

"I read about you online," Ahaan admitted, his smile widening. "I googled you last night and found your social media profiles. Your work is truly inspiring."

Aliza felt a chill run down her spine. The idea that Ahaan had looked her up online felt invasive and unsettling. "So, you decided to follow us and do some research on me?"

"I didn't mean to come across as creepy," Ahaan said, his tone still friendly. "I was genuinely interested in learning more about you after our encounter last night. I apologize if it seemed intrusive."

Nadeem, sensing Aliza's discomfort, stepped in. "Ahaan, we appreciate your interest, but I think it would be best if you gave us some space. We've had a long morning and would like to enjoy the rest of our day in peace."

Ahaan's smile finally faltered a bit. "Of course, I understand. I didn't mean to overstep. I'll leave you to your day."

He stood up, giving them one last smile before walking away. As he disappeared into the crowd, Aliza let out a sigh of relief.

"That guy gives me the creeps," she muttered.

Nadeem nodded in agreement. "He definitely seems a bit too eager. Let's just try to enjoy the rest of our day and forget about him."

They finished their breakfast in silence, both feeling a sense of unease. The morning had started off so beautifully, but Ahaan's intrusion had cast a shadow over their experience. Determined not to let it ruin their day, they paid the bill and set off to explore more of Varanasi.

The narrow lanes of the old city beckoned them with the promise of adventure. They wandered through bustling markets, filled with the scent of spices and the sound of merchants calling out their wares. They visited ancient places, where the air was thick with the nostalgic view of the old houses.

As they explored, Aliza found herself gradually relaxing. The vibrant energy of the city was infectious, and she couldn't help but be drawn into its charm. Nadeem, sensing her mood lift, suggested they take a boat ride to see the ghats from the river once more.

Back on the boat, the gentle rocking of the water and the serene beauty of the ghats helped to wash away the tension. They marveled at the sights, taking in the intricate architecture and the daily life unfolding along the riverbanks.

As they passed by Manikarnika Ghat again, they remembered the boat owner's caution from the previous night. They silently paid their respects, understanding the sanctity of the place and the traditions that surrounded it.

The boat ride was a perfect antidote to the earlier encounter. By the time they returned to the shore, Aliza felt rejuvenated, her earlier irritation completely forgotten.

"Let's make the most of our time here," Nadeem said, his voice filled with determination. "We can't let one person ruin our experience."

Aliza smiled, feeling a renewed sense of adventure. "You're right. Varanasi has so much to offer. Let's dive in and see everything this city has to show us."

As they continued their boat ride, the calmness of the river and the beauty of the ghats enveloped them. It was as though the waves were talking to one another.

They soaked in the peaceful atmosphere, appreciating the history and spirituality that surrounded them. Just as they were starting to forget about Ahaan, they heard a familiar voice from the boat next to their own.

"Hey!" Ahaan shouted, waving enthusiastically. He had a wide grin over his face. He was shining in the early morning's sun's ray and Aliza found that quite appealing for a while but then she controlled her emotions and reacted as she had to towards a stranger.

Aliza turned towards him, her irritation flaring up again. "Why are you following us?" she yelled, her voice echoing across the water.

Ahaan shrugged, still smiling. "I'm not following you! You both just seem to be everywhere I am. It's quite the coincidence," he said, chuckling. "And now look, we're on neighboring boats!"

Aliza's irritation was palpable. "We don't need your company, Ahaan," she snapped. "Can't you see we want to be left alone?"

Ahaan, seemingly unbothered, continued in his cheerful tone. "Hey, let's forget the tension among us and why don't we go to the other side of the river? There's a spot where you can take camel rides. It's a lot of fun!"

Nadeem's eyes lit up at the mention of camel rides. "That sounds interesting," he said, looking at Aliza. "I've always wanted to try a camel ride."

Aliza turned towards Nadeem and frowned. "Nadeem, we don't need to go where he suggests. We can find our own places to explore. I don't want this man to dictate what to do and what not."

Nadeem's enthusiasm didn't waver. "Come on, Aliza. You can't let this one guy ruin our trip. Camel rides sound like a unique experience. Let's give it a shot."

Aliza sighed, feeling cornered. She didn't want to let Ahaan dictate their plans, but she also didn't want to dampen Nadeem's excitement. "Fine," she relented, "but let's make it quick."

Ahaan, hearing their decision, smirked broadly. "Great! Follow me!" he shouted, guiding his boat towards the other side of the river.

As they crossed the river, Aliza couldn't shake off her annoyance. She muttered under her breath, "This better be worth it."

When they reached the other side, they saw a line of camels waiting along the shore, their handlers ready to assist tourists. The scene was picturesque, with the camels silhouetted against the rising sun and the river glistening behind them.

Nadeem hopped off the boat, his excitement palpable. "This is going to be amazing!" he said, turning to help Aliza disembark.

Aliza, still wary, let Nadeem lead her towards the camels. Ahaan was already there, chatting with one of the handlers and securing a camel for himself.

"Here we go," Ahaan said, mounting his camel with ease. "Let's explore the desert side of Varanasi!"

"These are no deserts. This is just the riverbed." Aliza claimed and then made a face of false irritation.

Nadeem climbed onto a camel, grinningly. "Come on, Aliza. It'll be fun."

With a resigned sigh, Aliza allowed one of the handlers to help her onto a camel. As they started their ride, she couldn't help but feel a small thrill of adventure. The gentle sway of the camel and the unique perspective it offered were unlike anything she had experienced before.

As they rode through the sandy terrain, Ahaan kept up a steady stream of conversation, pointing out interesting sights and sharing anecdotes. Despite herself, Aliza found some of his stories amusing, and Nadeem's enthusiasm was contagious.

"See, this isn't so bad," Nadeem said, flashing a smile at Aliza. "I'm glad we did this."

Aliza managed a small smile in return. "I suppose it's not the worst way to spend a morning."

As they continued their ride, the initial tension began to dissipate. Aliza found herself enjoying the experience more than she had anticipated. The landscape was beautiful, and the novelty of the camel ride added a sense of adventure to their day. They clicked many pictures but kept Ahaan away from the pictures as Aliza instructed Nadeem.

When they finally returned to the riverbank, Aliza felt a bit more at ease. She still didn't fully trust Ahaan, but she couldn't deny that the camel ride had been a memorable experience.

"Thanks for the suggestion, Ahaan," Nadeem said, dismounting his camel. "That was a lot of fun."

Ahaan beamed. "I'm glad you enjoyed it. Varanasi has so much to offer, and sometimes it's the unexpected experiences that make the best memories."

Aliza nodded reluctantly. "I guess you were right about that," she added, then took a deep breath. "And now we should move on to wherever we want. It was nice talking to you, but I think it would be better if we part our ways from here."

Ahaan ignored Aliza's pointed remark and turned to Nadeem with an enthusiastic grin. "Aren't you hungry? I know a place with the best spiced stuffed fritter nearby at the India's Fritter (Kachori) Center. Let's go there and have snacks."

Nadeem hesitated, glancing at Aliza. He could see she was still uncomfortable with Ahaan's presence, but the idea of trying the best spiced stuffed fritters in Varanasi was tempting.

"Come on, Nadeem," Ahaan continued, undeterred by Aliza's cool demeanor. "It's just a quick snack, and I promise you won't regret it. This place is legendary."

Aliza sighed, her patience wearing thin. "Nadeem, we don't have to go. We can find somewhere else."

Nadeem looked at Aliza, then back at Ahaan. "I really want to try those spiced stuffed fritters, Aliza. It's just a snack. We can go our own way after that."

Aliza felt cornered but decided to compromise for Nadeem's sake. "Fine," she said, her voice tight. "But after the quick snack, we're on our own."

Ahaan clapped his hands together. "Great! Follow me, it's just a short walk from here."

As they made their way through the bustling streets of Varanasi, the morning sunbathed the city in a warm glow. The aroma of street food filled the air, mingling with the scent of oil from the nearby cosmetic shops. Despite her irritation, Aliza couldn't help but feel a sense of wonder at the vibrant energy around her.

They arrived at a small, unassuming stall tucked away in a narrow alley. The stall owner greeted Ahaan with a nod, and within minutes, they were seated at a small table, steaming plates of spiced stuffed fritters in front of them.

"Trust me, these are the best," Ahaan said, taking a big bite and sighing with satisfaction.

Nadeem followed suit, his eyes widening with delight. "Wow, these are incredible!"

Aliza took a tentative bite, and despite her reservations, she had to admit they were delicious. The crispy outer layer gave way to a flavorful, spicy filling that was both satisfying and comforting.

For a few moments, the tension eased as they focused on their meal. Ahaan kept the conversation light, sharing stories about his travels and the history of Varanasi. Nadeem seemed genuinely interested, but Aliza remained guarded, unwilling to fully let her guard down.

As they finished their breakfast, Ahaan leaned back with a contented sigh. "See? I told you it would be worth it."

Nadeem nodded. "You were right. Thanks for bringing us here."

Aliza forced a polite smile. "Yes, thank you. Now, if you don't mind, we'd like to continue exploring on our own."

Ahaan raised his hands in a gesture of surrender. "Of course, of course. I don't want to intrude. Enjoy the rest of your day."

Aliza and Nadeem stood up to leave, and Ahaan watched them go, a thoughtful expression crossing his face. Suddenly, he seemed to decide. "But before you go..." Ahaan started, but Aliza quickly stepped forward, taking Ahaan by the arm and pulling him away from Nadeem. She wanted to confront him alone.

"Okay, mister, now you are irritating me," Aliza said, her voice low but firm. "I know what you're doing. Stop playing these funny games. I know what kind of person you are and how you think I'll respond to your so-called cute antics. This isn't a Bollywood movie, so please, go away or I'll call the police."

Ahaan smiled, unfazed by her words. "What will you tell the police?" he asked, his tone light and mocking. "That I took you on a camel ride and made you eat spiced stuffed fritters forcefully? Don't be ridiculous. I'm just looking for some company. Nadeem seems like a nice guy, and you're just taking everything too seriously. Just relax."

Aliza felt her anger flare, but she also felt something else—a strange, unwelcome sensation as she looked into Ahaan's eyes. There was a moment, a fleeting second, where she felt a tickling sensation inside her, almost like she was falling for him. But she quickly forced herself to ignite her anger again, refusing to let her guard down.

"I don't need to relax," she snapped. "I need you to leave us alone." She turned on her heel and marched back to Nadeem, her heart pounding in her chest.

Nadeem looked at her with concern. "What did he say?"

"Nothing important," Aliza replied, her voice tight. "Let's just go."

Ahaan saw both of them leaving. He had a smile on his face. He knew this wasn't the last goodbye. He had a lot of things to do together with Aliza. He simply followed her and took the next taxi to the destination where Aliza was heading. he planned his next move on the move. He knew where Aliza was heading. He knew what he had to do to please the girl.

5 - The Plan

Ahaan knew that Aliza would go to the local bookstore next. He had researched everything about her meticulously, piecing together her routines, likes, and dislikes from the digital breadcrumbs she left behind. Authors and writers are a unique breed, often caught between the solitary world of their craft and the need to remain visible in the public eye. In today's age, this visibility often comes from an active and engaging social media presence. They need to attract attention on social media platforms, or else they risk fading into obscurity. Their careers thrive on the buzz created by followers, likes, and shares, and to maintain this, they share everything about themselves online.

Aliza, being an author, was no exception. She posted about her book signings, her favourite writing spots, snippets of her daily life, and even the little things that inspired her creativity. Her Instagram was filled with pictures of her favourite cafes, snapshots of book covers, and candid moments of her writing process. Her Twitter was a mix of promotional content, interactions with fans, and musings on various topics. From these posts, Ahaan gleaned not just her public persona but glimpses of her private world.

He knew she had a deep love for literature, a penchant for quaint, independent bookstores, and a routine that often led her to such places whenever she travelled. Her recent posts about Varanasi had included mentions of the city's historic ghats, the mesmerizing Ganga Ceremony, and a specific bookstore that she couldn't wait to visit. This bookstore, she had written, was a hidden gem, a place where she could lose herself among the stacks of old, rare books.

Ahaan's plan was meticulous. He understood that to get closer to Aliza, he needed to show interest in what she loved, to create opportunities where their paths would cross naturally. He wanted to appear as more than just a chance encounter but as someone who shared her interests and passions. The bookstore was the perfect place for this.

As he rode in the taxi through the bustling streets of Varanasi, he felt a mixture of anticipation and determination. He rehearsed his approach in his mind, planning how he would engage her in conversation without seeming intrusive.

When Aliza and Nadeem arrived at the bookstore, Ahaan stayed back, watching them through the window. Aliza's face lit up as she entered, her earlier frustration dissipating in the comforting embrace of bookshelves lined with literary treasures. The bookstore was charming, with wooden shelves packed tightly with books, the air rich with the smell of aged paper and ink. Soft classical music played in the background, adding to the serene atmosphere.

Aliza wandered through the aisles, her fingers trailing along the spines of books, her mind engrossed in the world of words and stories. Nadeem, sensing her need for some alone time, moved to a different section, leaving Aliza to her thoughts. As she explored the store, Aliza did what all authors do upon entering a bookstore: she looked for her own book.

She navigated through the fiction section, scanning the shelves meticulously. However, after several minutes of searching, she couldn't find a single copy of her book. This was unusual. She was a bestselling author, and there wasn't a store in India that didn't have at least one copy of her book. She felt that her frustration was now coming back to her, and she could feel it rising in her veins.

Aliza approached the shop owner, a middle-aged man with a kind face and glasses perched on the bridge of his nose. He looked up from his ledger as she approached. He had a smile that was quite good to melt anyone's heart, but Aliza had something else in her mind.

"Excuse me," Aliza said politely, hiding her anger. "I was looking for my book, but I can't seem to find it. It's usually here."

The shop owner didn't get what Aliza meant, she then explained.

"Sorry I forgot to introduce myself. I am Aliza, the author."

The shop owner smiled warmly. "What's the title of your book?"

"'Aliza's Memoirs'" by Aliza Khan," she replied, her voice tinged with a hint of frustration and curiosity. The shop owner had no idea about her and that was quite unusual for her. That was a quite serious blow to her ego.

The shop owner's eyes lit up with recognition. "Ah, yes, Aliza Khan. I know your work well. We had several copies of your book."

"Had?" Aliza echoed, puzzled. "What happened to them?"

The shop owner chuckled softly. "You're not going to believe this, but just this morning, someone came in and bought every single copy we had."

Aliza's eyebrows shot up in surprise. "All of them? Who would buy that many copies?"

The shop owner shrugged. "I didn't get his name, but he seemed very enthusiastic about your work. Said he was a big fan and wanted to give them as gifts."

Aliza felt a mixture of emotions—flattered, confused, and slightly uneasy. "Well, that's... unexpected. Thank you for letting me know."

As she turned away, she couldn't help but wonder about the mysterious buyer. Her mind raced with possibilities, but one name kept coming back to her: Ahaan. She shook her head, trying to dismiss the thought, but a nagging suspicion lingered. But why would he do that? Another coincidence?

She rejoined Nadeem, who was browsing through a section of travel guides. "Hey, found anything interesting?" he asked, glancing up.

Aliza hesitated, then decided to share. "Apparently, someone bought all the copies of my book this morning."

Nadeem raised an eyebrow. "Really? That's strange. Who would do that?"

Aliza sighed. "The shop owner didn't know. He said it was some enthusiastic fan."

Nadeem looked thoughtful. "Do you think it could be...?"

Aliza nodded slowly. She had a puzzled look on her face. "Yeah, I think it might be Ahaan."

Nadeem frowned. "Why would he do that?"

"I'm not sure," Aliza admitted. "But I have a feeling we're going to find out soon enough."

As Aliza stepped out of the bookstore, she noticed a quaint tea shop nestled at the corner of the street. The shop exuded an inviting charm, its warm glow spilling out onto the sidewalk, where clusters of students and collegegoers animatedly chatted and laughed. The air was filled with the rich aroma of brewing tea and freshly baked pastries. Drawn by the lively atmosphere and the comforting scents, Aliza made her way over, feeling a sense of excitement bubbling within her.

Pushing open the door, she was greeted by a cozy interior,

adorned with mismatched chairs and wooden tables, each bearing the marks of countless conversations and shared moments. Strings of fairy lights hung from the ceiling, casting a soft, twinkling glow across the room. The walls were lined with colourful posters and artworks, and a small stage in the corner suggested that live performances were a regular feature.

Aliza approached the counter and ordered a cup of masala chai, her favourite. As she waited, she let her eyes wander, taking in the vibrant scene around her. The shop was abuzz with the hum of conversation, the clinking of cups, and the rustle of pages turning. It was a haven of energy and creativity, and Aliza felt right at home.

Her gaze fell on the next table, where a student with a backpack slung over the chair was deeply engrossed in a book. Aliza's heart skipped a beat as she recognized the familiar cover—her book. A surge of pride and warmth washed over her, and she couldn't help but smile.

As she continued to scan the room, she noticed another student at a different table, also reading her book, their brow furrowed in concentration. Aliza's smile widened. She looked around more carefully and realized that several students throughout the shop were reading her book, all dressed in the same school uniform— a navy blazer with a crest on the pocket, white shirts, and neatly tied ties.

Her tea arrived, and she carried it to a small table near the window, still marvelling at the sight of so many students engaged with her work. She took a seat and sipped her tea, the warm, spicy liquid providing a comforting contrast to the cool morning air.

As she sat there, basking in the moment, a young woman with glasses and a bright smile caught her eye. The student's eyes widened in recognition, and she whispered excitedly to her friends before getting up and approaching Aliza with a mix of shyness and awe.

"Excuse me, are you Aliza Khan?" the student asked, her voice tinged with excitement.

Aliza smiled warmly. "Yes, I am."

The student's face lit up. "I can't believe it! I'm a huge fan of your work. Could I please get your autograph?"

"Of course," Aliza replied, feeling a rush of joy. She took the book the student held out and signed it with a flourish. She had a great practice for all this. Giving autograph was not a new thing for her. "What's your name?"

"Ananya," the student replied, beaming with excitement that was visible on her face throughout. She was almost jumping of joy.

"Nice to meet you, Ananya," Aliza said, handing the book back. "I'm glad you enjoy my book. By the way, I noticed a lot of students here are reading it. Do you mind if I ask where you all got the copies?"

Ananya nodded eagerly. "Someone at our college gave them to us. He said he wanted to share a great book with everyone. We never had imagined that we'll be having a chat with the author as well. Why didn't you come to our college?"

Aliza's curiosity piqued. "I would definitely do that. Will ask my publisher to arrange something. By the way did he say who he was?"

"No, he didn't," Ananya said, shaking her head. "But he seemed really passionate about your work. He even organized a small reading group for us to discuss the book."

Aliza felt a mix of flattery and suspicion. "That's very kind of him. Thank you for letting me know, Ananya."

As Ananya returned to her table, Aliza sipped her tea, her mind racing. It seemed that Ahaan was determined to keep her in his sights, and his latest move had not only put her book in the hands of many readers but also drawn more attention to her. She couldn't help but wonder what his endgame was and how far he was willing to go to stay close to her.

Aliza leaned back in her chair, taking another sip of her tea. The shop buzzed around her, but her mind was elsewhere, grappling with the realization that Ahaan's intentions were more complex than they seemed. The sight of her book in so many hands was gratifying, yet the knowledge of Ahaan's involvement left her with a lingering sense of unease.

Determined to get to the bottom of this, Aliza decided to go to the college and find out who had distributed the books to the students. She gathered her belongings and left the tea shop, her heart set on uncovering the mystery.

The college was a short walk away, and as Aliza entered the bustling campus, she marvelled at the energy and enthusiasm of the students. She asked a few of them for directions to the principal's office, and they eagerly pointed her in the right direction, clearly recognizing her.

As she approached the office, Aliza took a deep breath, trying to steady her nerves. She knocked on the door and waited. A moment later, the door opened to reveal a middle-aged woman with kind eyes and a welcoming smile.

"Good morning," the principal said, her eyes widening in recognition. She was a dignified woman in her late forties, with neatly styled hair and a warm, inviting presence. Her office was adorned with certificates and photos of various school events, reflecting a career dedicated to education. "You must be Aliza

Khan. It's an honour to have you here. Please, come in."

Aliza felt a bit more at ease seeing the principal's genuine warmth. "Thank you," Aliza replied, stepping into the office. She glanced around, taking in the cozy but professional atmosphere, and noticed a shelf filled with books and awards, indicating the principal's passion for literature and academic excellence. "I hope I'm not intruding. I wanted to ask about something that happened recently."

"Of course," the principal said, gesturing for Aliza to take a seat. She moved with a grace that spoke of years of experience in handling various situations. The principal's desk was organized, with neatly stacked papers and a few personal trinkets, including a small framed picture of her family. "How can I help you?"

Aliza took a seat, her hands clasped in her lap. She felt a mixture of anticipation and curiosity. The chair was comfortable, and she took a moment to gather her thoughts, looking briefly out the window where students were mingling in the courtyard. "I noticed that many of your students are reading my book. I was curious about who distributed the copies."

The principal's expression turned thoughtful, and she nodded slowly. "Yes, we've had quite a buzz about your book lately. One of our teachers, Mr. Manav, distributed the copies. He's very passionate about literature and thought it would be a wonderful addition to our students' reading material."

Aliza's curiosity grew. "Mr. Manav, you said? Could you tell me more about him?" She was expecting the name of Ahaan but then realized he was a tourist and not a teacher here. How could she be that naive.

"Certainly," the principal replied, her tone warm and proud. "Mr. Manav is one of our English teachers. He's been with us for a few years now and is very well-liked by the students. He's always looking for ways to inspire them and broaden their horizons."

Aliza leaned forward slightly, intrigued. "Do you know where I might find him?" She really wanted to meet such a man who did such a big thing for her.

The principal checked her watch and smiled. "He should be in his classroom right now. It's just down the hall, Room 204. Would you like me to accompany you?"

Aliza appreciated the offer but shook her head gently. "That's very kind of you, but I can manage. Thank you for your help."

The principal stood as well and extended her hand, her expression sincere. "It was a pleasure meeting you, Ms. Khan. I hope you find what you're looking for. And one more thing, if you don't mind, can you join us in the morning assembly tomorrow? We would love to host you and introduce you formally with our students. I am sure some of them must have finished your book by then as well."

Aliza shook her hand, feeling a sense of camaraderie. "Thank you. It was nice meeting you too and I will definitely join. It would be great opportunity for me as well." She turned and walked out of the office, her mind racing with thoughts about Mr. Manav.

As she made her way down the hallway, the sounds of students chatting and laughing filled the air, creating a vibrant and lively atmosphere. Aliza found Room 204 and took a deep breath before knocking on the door. The door opened, revealing a classroom full of engaged students and a man at the front, mid-sentence.

Mr. Manav paused and looked up, his eyes meeting Aliza's. There was a moment of recognition, and then he smiled warmly. "Ms. Khan, what a surprise! This must be a lucky day for me. Please, come in.”

“Good morning,” Aliza replied, feeling a mix of apprehension and determination. “Are you Mr. Manav?”

“Yes, I am,” he replied, his eyes lighting up with recognition. “It’s an honour to meet you.”

“Thank you,” Aliza said, stepping into the classroom. “I wanted to ask you about the copies of my book that you distributed to the students. Can you tell me more about why you did that?”

Mr. Manav gestured to an empty chair at the front of the class. “Please, have a seat. I’d love to explain.”

Aliza took the seat, the students now paying close attention to the exchange. Mr. Manav continued, “Your book has had a profound impact on me personally, and I believe it has the potential to inspire my students as well. When I saw it at the bookstore, I knew I had to get copies for the class.”

Aliza raised an eyebrow. “And you bought all the copies?”

Mr. Manav nodded. “Yes, I wanted to make sure every student had the opportunity to read it. Your writing not only tells a compelling story but also touches on themes that are very relevant to our curriculum and to the students’ lives, moreover the content is very clean unlike the books of today’s world and you have passed on your message very nicely”.

“That’s unbelievable. I mean you really did that. I can’t believe this.” Aliza was shocked and elated.

Then Manav started to smile sheepishly.

“What happened?” Aliza was confused.

"I am really sorry, but I didn't buy all these books, and this was not my idea as well." He stopped for a while and then added, "Let me first explain. I am actually a very big fan of your writing, but all this was my friend's idea, and I am nowhere involved in it."

Manav hesitated for a moment and then added. "A friend of mine, Ahaan, mentioned that he had a few extra copies and offered to donate them to the school. I thought it was a generous gesture, and I didn't see any harm in it. And he was the one who called me just a few minutes ago and told me to pull this prank on you."

Aliza's heart sank. So, Ahaan was involved after all. She forced a smile and said, "Thank you for your honesty, Mr. Manav. Now I think I should leave. I am already tired of this man… this friend of yours. If you meet him, just tell him that please don't follow me, don't come across my path and don't come in front of my eyes as well. Will you please do that for me?"

Aliza said and left the classroom, her mind swirling with anger. As she made her way back to the main campus, she couldn't shake the feeling that Ahaan's intentions were doubtful. She saw Nadeem waiting patiently outside the college campus. She walked towards him and then saw Ahaan standing next to Nadeem.

6 - The First Formal Introduction

Her fury ignited; Aliza marched up to Ahaan without a second thought. "What is wrong with you?" she shouted, not caring about the curious onlookers. "Why can't you just leave us alone? First, you buy all the copies of my book, and now you're here, lurking around! What game are you playing?"

Ahaan remained silent, his expression calm as he let Aliza vent her frustration. Nadeem looked from Aliza to Ahaan, unsure of what to say.

Aliza continued, her voice trembling with anger. "Do you think this is funny? Do you think stalking us and pretending to be some kind of... fan is acceptable behavior? You have no right to invade our lives like this!"

"Hey Mister, let me tell you one thing, your cheap tricks are not going to work on me. I know you care nothing about Literature and arts and whatever you are doing to show that you love my writing and you are my fan, just chuck it out. I know the fraudsters like you. Just leave us alone." Aliza shouted on Ahaan at the top of her lungs.

There was a pause as Aliza caught her breath. Ahaan finally spoke, his tone gentle and completely unexpected. "Would you like to have an ice cream?"

Aliza blinked, momentarily thrown off balance by the absurdity of the question. "What?"

Ahaan smiled, unfazed by her outburst. "An ice cream. There's a great place just around the corner. Sometimes, a little sweetness can help calm the storm inside."

Aliza stared at him, her anger mingling with confusion. She hadn't expected such a response. Nadeem, sensing an opportunity to diffuse the situation, chimed in, "Maybe we should all take a break. An ice cream doesn't sound like a bad idea, does it, Aliza?" Nadeem knew that Aliza wouldn't say no to ice cream, even if she is angry.

She sighed, her shoulders slumping slightly. "Fine. But this doesn't mean I'm okay with everything you've done, Ahaan."

Ahaan nodded, his smile never wavering. "Understood. Let's go."

As they walked towards the ice cream shop, Aliza couldn't help but feel a strange mixture of irritation and curiosity about Ahaan. She couldn't shake the feeling that there was more to his actions than met the eye, and part of her was determined to find out what it was.

Once inside the shop, Aliza ordered herself a chocolate cone, while Nadeem chose a vanilla one. Ahaan opted for a strawberry-flavored cup. They found a quiet corner to sit, and for a few minutes, they ate in silence, the only sounds being the occasional clink of Ahaan's spoon against his cup.

Finally, Aliza couldn't hold back any longer. "Why are you doing all this?" she asked, her tone blunt and direct.

Ahaan looked up from his ice cream, a playful smile on his lips. "Because I think I love you."

Aliza blinked, stunned into silence.

"I've known about you from social media," Ahaan continued, undeterred by Aliza's reaction. "I find you cute, interesting, and I admire your work. I'm single at the moment, and I know you are as well. You might be wondering how I can say I like you without really knowing you, so let me introduce myself properly."

He leaned back, adopting a mock-serious tone. "I am Ahaan, 28 years old, from Delhi. I did my graduation in arts and I'm a poet by profession. I'm 5'9", weigh about 70 kilos, and I've been told my complexion is 'wheatish,' whatever that means. My hobbies include long walks on the beach, serenading strangers, and apparently, annoying bestselling authors and people around me say that I am very handsome and adorable".

Nadeem snorted into his ice cream, trying to suppress his laughter. Aliza, despite herself, felt a small smile tug at the corners of her mouth.

Ahaan continued, his expression earnest now. "I know this might seem strange, but I really wanted to meet you and get to know you better. Maybe I'm going about it the wrong way, but my intentions are genuine. I promise."

Aliza studied him for a moment, trying to gauge his sincerity. "This isn't some kind of elaborate joke, is it?"

Ahaan shook his head. "No joke. Just a guy trying to make a connection in the best way he knows how. Even if that way is a bit... unconventional."

Aliza sighed, her irritation slowly giving way to curiosity. "Alright, Ahaan. You've got my attention. Now tell me what you want?"

Ahaan looked at her earnestly. "Didn't I just tell you I like you? And I told you everything about me as well. What else do you want to know?"

Aliza raised an eyebrow. "Is that all you think a girl wants to know before falling in love?"

Ahaan looked thoughtful for a moment. "So, what do you want from me?"

There was a silence for a while, the only sound being the soft chatter of the shop around them. Then Nadeem, sensing an opportunity to lighten the mood, spoke up. "You said you are a poet. Recite a poetry for her."

Ahaan looked around; a bit hesitant. "Here, right now?"

Aliza, her curiosity piqued, challenged him with a playful smirk. "Are you afraid? Or maybe not that good at your art?"

Ahaan paused for a moment, then took a deep breath and stood up. He cleared his throat and began to recite, his voice soft and melodious:

> In streets of stone, where whispers meet,
> A hush descends, a magic sweet.
> There dwells a vision, fair and bright,
> Aliza named, a bright sunlit light.
>
> Her name, a sigh on lips that yearn,
> A melody the heavens learn.
> Each step a pause, the world in thrall,
> As light from her begins to fall.
>
> A beauty born of purest grace,
> Not just of form, but heart's embrace.
> Hazel eyes, a sunlit dream,
> Where galaxies in starlight gleam.
>
> A thousand tales within them lie,
> Of destinies that intertwine.
> Poets strive, with words in vain,
> To capture fire that burns like rain.
>
> Her hair, a cascade spun of gold,
> A moonlit river, soft and bold.
> With every breeze, it seems to sing,

Of secrets whispered, legends cling.

But oh, the dimple on her cheek,
A secret pact the heavens seek.
It holds the laughter, light and free,
A glimpse of joy eternally.

For Aliza's beauty, rare and deep,
Is not a gift the senses keep.
It's strength that shines, a hope untold,
A spirit both luminous, and bold.

As pages turn, her story unfolds,
A beauty more than what it holds.
It's light within, a radiant soul,
That makes Aliza truly whole.

As he continued with his poem his voice grew stronger in confidence, filling the small ice cream shop. The crowd of students and collegegoers around them began to quiet down, their attention drawn to Ahaan's impromptu performance. People started to gather closer, forming a small circle around their table. The group of collegegoers pulled out the chairs from the adjoining tables and shifted them closer to Ahaan's chair.

The ambiance of the shop transformed. The background noise of casual conversations and clinking cups faded away, replaced by the smooth, soulful notes of Ahaan's poem. The soft, warm light of the shop created an almost magical atmosphere, casting a gentle glow on Ahaan as he recited with heartfelt emotion.

Aliza watched in amazement, her irritation melting away as she got lost in the moment. There was something undeniably captivating about Ahaan's crisp voice, the way it conveyed a depth of feeling that words alone could not express.

The poem ended, and for a moment, there was a stunned silence.

Then, the crowd erupted into applause, cheers, and whistles. Ahaan took a modest bow, a shy smile playing on his lips. He glanced at Aliza, who was clapping along with everyone else, her eyes shining with a mix of surprise and admiration.

Ahaan sat back down, the crowd slowly dispersing but still buzzing with excitement. He looked at Aliza, his expression earnest. "So, what do you think?"

Aliza couldn't help but smile. "That was... beautiful. I didn't expect that."

Nadeem, grinningly, nudged Aliza. "See? Not so bad after all."

Aliza, feeling her irritation soften into genuine curiosity, nodded. "Yeah, not bad at all."

Ahaan's eyes sparkled with hope. "I'm glad you think so. How about we catch a movie together?"

Aliza shook her head, though her smile remained. "No, we have some work to do."

Ahaan leaned in; his tone playful yet sincere. "If you don't come with me, how will you know who I really am? Let's roam around and explore. Let's get to know each other better."

Nadeem, ever the mediator, chimed in. "I know you both have no real work to do right now. Let's go and watch a movie. It'll be fun!"

Aliza hesitated for a moment, then laughed. "Alright, alright. You two win. Let's go watch a movie."

Ahaan's face lit up with a wide grin. "Great! I promise, it'll be worth it."

As they left the shop and made their way to the nearby cinema, Aliza couldn't help but feel a sense of excitement and anticipation. The day had taken an unexpected turn, but maybe, just maybe, it was leading to something good.

Nadeem walked besides them; his excitement palpable. "What kind of movie are we watching? Romance? Comedy? Action?"

Ahaan looked at Aliza. "Your choice, Aliza. What do you feel like watching?"

Aliza thought for a moment, then smiled. "How about a light-hearted comedy? Something fun."

"Comedy it is," Ahaan agreed. "Let's make it a memorable day."

As they settled into their seats at the theater, Aliza found herself relaxing more and more. Maybe getting to know Ahaan wouldn't be so bad after all. Maybe, this spontaneous adventure could lead to something wonderful. The theater was dimly lit, and the previews were just starting to play.

Nadeem, leaning closer to his sister, whispered in her ear, "I know you are enjoying this, but keep that stern face on. No need to melt so quickly."

Aliza looked at her brother in amazement, a mixture of amusement and annoyance in her eyes. "Shut up, Nadeem," she whispered back, a smile tugging at the corners of her lips. She tried to keep her composure, but she was genuinely enjoying the experience.

The movie started, and the three of them settled into their seats, the flickering light of the screen illuminating their faces. Aliza found herself laughing at the funny moments, her earlier tension melting away with each passing minute. Ahaan, sitting next to her, glanced over occasionally, pleased to see her smiling and relaxed.

Halfway through the movie, there was a particularly hilarious scene that had the entire audience roaring with laughter. Aliza glanced at Ahaan and caught him looking at her. Their eyes met, and for a brief moment, they shared a silent connection, an understanding that maybe this unexpected encounter was meant to be.

Nadeem, noticing the exchange, couldn't help but tease his sister again. "Enjoying the movie, huh?"

Aliza playfully elbowed him. "Quiet, you. Just watch the movie."

As the film continued, Aliza felt a warmth spreading through her, a feeling of contentment that she hadn't experienced in a long time. She realized that she was no longer just tolerating Ahaan's presence; she was genuinely enjoying it. His spontaneous nature, which had initially annoyed her, now seemed endearing and refreshing.

When the credits finally rolled, the lights came up, and the audience began to file out of the theater. Ahaan turned to Aliza with a hopeful smile. "So, what did you think? Was it worth it?"

Aliza nodded; her smile genuine. "Yes, it was. Thank you, Ahaan."

Nadeem, ever the cheeky brother, added, "See? I told you it would be fun."

The three of them walked out of the theater together, the evening air cool and refreshing. Aliza felt a sense of anticipation for what the rest of the day might hold. As they strolled down the street, Ahaan suggested, "How about we grab some dinner? There's a great restaurant just around the corner."

"How do you know everything about this city?" Aliza asked, curious.

Ahaan smiled, a hint of nostalgia in his eyes. "I was born in Varanasi. My father was in the army, and we moved to Delhi when I was young. But I spent my early years here, so this city is like a second home to me."

As they strolled down the bustling street, the sun began to set, casting a warm, golden glow over the city. The air was filled with the rich aroma of street food and the distant hum of conversations and laughter. Aliza glanced around, taking in the vibrant surroundings, before turning her attention back to Ahaan.

"Is your father retired now?" Aliza inquired, her voice gentle.

Ahaan's smile faded slightly, but he maintained his composure, the setting sun casting long shadows across his face. "No, he passed away. He died in the Kargil War."

"I'm sorry," Aliza said softly, feeling a pang of sympathy as they passed a group of children playing near a small park. The children's laughter echoed through the air, a stark contrast to the somber moment.

Ahaan nodded, his expression solemn but proud, illuminated by the golden light. "Thank you. I'm proud of my dad. He was a brave man."

They walked in silence for a moment, the sounds of the city enveloping them. Aliza hoped to shift the conversation to a lighter topic. "So, what does your mother do?" she asked, her curiosity piqued.

"She's a housewife," Ahaan replied, his smile returning as they neared a quaint restaurant with twinkling fairy lights. "But she also works with a charitable organization that helps underprivileged kids. She's dedicated her life to making a difference in their lives."

"That's wonderful," Aliza said, genuinely impressed as they stepped into the cozy restaurant. The warm interior, filled with the scent of freshly cooked food and the soft murmur of diners, provided a welcoming atmosphere. "It sounds like she's an amazing woman."

"She is," Ahaan agreed, his eyes reflecting the twinkling lights. "I've learned a lot from her. She's taught me the importance of giving back and helping others."

As they settled into a corner booth by the window, the city lights twinkling outside, Aliza felt a deeper connection forming with Ahaan. The waiter brought the menu, and they continued their conversation, sharing stories and laughter, creating a memorable evening that neither of them would soon forget.

Nadeem, always the icebreaker, picked up the menu and said, "So, what's good here, Ahaan?"

"Everything," Ahaan said with a grin. "But I highly recommend the paneer tikka and the butter chicken. They make it really well here."

They ordered their food and continued their conversation, sharing stories and laughter. Aliza found herself relaxing more and more, enjoying the company and the unexpected turn of events.

As the evening wore on, Aliza couldn't help but feel grateful for this day. Meeting Ahaan, learning about his life, and seeing the world through his eyes had been a refreshing change. She realized that sometimes, stepping out of her comfort zone could lead to wonderful experiences and connections.

When their food arrived, the conversation continued to flow easily. Ahaan's charm and genuine nature made Aliza feel comfortable and appreciated. They shared stories about their childhoods, their dreams, and their passions.

"So, Aliza," Ahaan said, looking at her with genuine curiosity, his eyes reflecting the dim light of the cozy café they were sitting in. "I know this question sounds very cliché, but still, what inspired you to become a writer?"

Aliza smiled, her thoughts drifting back to her childhood. "I've always loved stories," she began, her voice softening with nostalgia. "Ever since I was a little girl, I would get lost in books. I remember hiding under the covers with a flashlight, reading late into the night, completely engrossed in the adventures and lives of the characters. Writing was my way of creating my own worlds and sharing them with others. It's my passion."

Ahaan nodded, clearly impressed. He leaned forward, resting his chin on his hand, his interest evident. "That's amazing. Your stories have a way of touching people's hearts. I can see why you're so successful."

"Thank you," Aliza replied, feeling a warmth spread through her. "It means a lot to hear that. Sometimes, writing can feel like such a solitary endeavour. You spend so much time alone with your thoughts, and you can't always be sure that what you're creating will resonate with others."

Ahaan's eyes sparkled with understanding. "I can imagine. But you've definitely struck a chord with your readers. What was the first story you ever wrote?"

Aliza laughed, her eyes lighting up with amusement. "Oh, it was a very simple story about a little girl who wanted to fly. I must have been about seven or eight years old. I wrote it in a notebook with a glittery cover and illustrated it with coloured pencils. My parents were my first audience, and they were so encouraging. They made me believe that I could be a writer one day."

"That sounds adorable," Ahaan said with a chuckle. "Do you still have that notebook?"

"I do, actually," Aliza said, her smile growing wider. "It's tucked away in a box of childhood memories. It's a reminder of where I started and how far I've come."

Ahaan leaned back in his chair, looking thoughtful. "It's incredible how those early experiences shape us. Do you ever go back to that box for inspiration?"

"Sometimes," Aliza admitted. "When I'm feeling stuck or doubting myself, I go back and read those old stories. They remind me of the pure joy I felt when I first started writing. It helps me reconnect with that sense of wonder and possibility."

Ahaan nodded, his admiration for Aliza evident. "That's such a beautiful way to stay connected to your roots. Do you have any specific themes or messages that you hope to convey through your writing?"

Aliza took a moment to consider his question. "I think the most important thing for me is to tell stories that feel real and honest. I want my readers to see themselves in my characters, to feel understood and less alone. Whether it's through joy, sorrow, love, or loss, I want to capture the full spectrum of human experience."

"Well, you certainly do that," Ahaan said, his voice sincere. "Your characters are so relatable and your stories so moving. It's no wonder you have such a dedicated following."

Nadeem, who had been listening quietly, chimed in. "Aliza's always been the creative one in the family. I'm more of the practical type." He joked just to bring himself into the conversation.

"Every family needs a balance," Ahaan said with a smile. "And it's clear you two have a great bond."

As the night ended, Aliza felt a sense of contentment. This unexpected day had turned out to be one of the most memorable experiences she had in a long time. She looked at Ahaan and realized that sometimes, taking a chance on the unknown could lead to something truly special.

*****

Aliza sat down on her chair, feeling the weight of another unproductive day pressing down on her shoulders. The main reason for visiting Varanasi was not to explore the city but to find the muse to write. This ancient city, with its labyrinthine alleys, ghats, and spiritual aura, seemed like the perfect place to ignite her creativity. But nothing was coming to her. She had been sitting in front of her laptop for hours, staring at the blinking cursor on a blank page, her mind a frustratingly empty slate.

She began typing, hoping to force her thoughts into some semblance of order. A few sentences formed, but they felt forced, lifeless. Sighing, she leaned back in her chair, her fingers pausing over the keyboard. Instead of the flow of ideas she had hoped for, her mind was filled with the events of the day and, most persistently, thoughts of Ahaan.

Ahaan. Just thinking his name brought a smile to her lips. She replayed their encounters in her mind: the ice cream shop, the unexpected poem recitation, the shared dinner at the cozy restaurant. His voice reciting the poem echoed in her memory, soft and soothing. His stories about his father, a brave soldier who died in the Kargil War, and his mother, a dedicated woman working with a charitable organization, painted a picture of a man with depth and a kind heart.

Aliza shook her head, trying to refocus on her writing. She placed her fingers on the keyboard once more, determined to push through the block. But the words wouldn't come. Every attempt felt stilted, devoid of the passion and life she wanted to convey. Frustrated, she closed the lid of her laptop with a soft click and reached for her diary instead.

The diary's leather cover was worn from years of use, its pages filled with her thoughts, dreams, and experiences. Aliza found comfort in the familiar feel of it. She opened it to a fresh page, picked up her pen, and began to write.

Dear Diary # 1

Dear Diary,

Today has been a whirlwind, and as I sit here reflecting on everything that transpired, I feel an overwhelming sense of gratitude and bewilderment. There's so much to unpack, and my thoughts are a tangled mess of emotions. It all started so ordinarily but evolved into something truly extraordinary, something that has left an indelible mark on my heart.

I began my day wandering through the bookstore, lost in the familiar comfort of words and stories. Nadeem, sensing my need for solitude, drifted away to another section, giving me the space I needed. That's when I noticed something unusual – my book was missing from the shelves. The shopkeeper's explanation that all copies had just sold out, and the knowledge that someone had bought them all, filled me with curiosity and a strange sense of foreboding. That someone turned out to be Ahaan, the enigmatic man who had been weaving in and out of my day in ways I hadn't anticipated. We crossed paths again, and this time, I confronted him, letting all my frustration pour out. He stood there, silent and composed, his eyes reflecting a depth I hadn't seen before. And then, with a simple yet unexpected gesture, he asked if I'd like to have ice cream. It was such an innocent, almost childlike offer that it caught me off guard and, surprisingly, diffused my anger.

As we walked to the ice cream shop, something about Ahaan began to intrigue me. There was a genuineness to him, a sincerity that I couldn't ignore. He spoke about his life in a way that was both open and endearing. Learning about his father's sacrifice in the Kargil War and his mother's dedication to helping underprivileged children painted a picture of a man shaped by love, loss, and a deep sense of responsibility.

When we sat in the ice cream shop, the atmosphere buzzing with the chatter and laughter of other patrons, I felt a shift within myself. I ordered a chocolate cone, Nadeem chose vanilla, and Ahaan opted for a strawberry cup. We ate in silence at first, but it wasn't uncomfortable. It felt like the calm before a storm, a moment of quiet reflection before diving into deeper waters.

And then came the question that had been gnawing at me: "Why are you doing all this?" His answer, so straightforward and heartfelt, left me momentarily speechless. He confessed his feelings in a way that was both candid and vulnerable, revealing his admiration for me gleaned from social media. He shared snippets of his life – his age, his background, his profession as a poet – with a blend of humor and earnestness that was disarming.

Nadeem's suggestion for Ahaan to recite the poem took the day to another level entirely. Amidst the curious onlookers and the ambient noises of the city, Ahaan began to recite his poem. His voice was like a gentle breeze, carrying the melody with such grace and emotion that it captivated everyone around. The crowd gathered, drawn by the beauty of his performance, and for those few moments, it felt like the world had stopped spinning. His voice, rich and melodious, conveyed a depth of feeling that words alone couldn't capture. As we walked out of the theater later, Ahaan suggested dinner, and his familiarity with the city added another layer to his charm. The way he spoke about his past, his father's legacy, and his mother's work with a charitable organization, painted a picture of a man deeply rooted in values and driven by a desire to make a positive impact. His humility and the pride he felt for his family were evident in every word he spoke.

Dinner was a continuation of this unfolding story. The restaurant, cozy and warm, felt like a haven. Our conversation flowed effortlessly, punctuated by laughter and shared stories. I found myself drawn to Ahaan's passion and his genuine interest in making the world a better place. He had a way of looking at things, at people, that was both profound and refreshing. His perspectives were thoughtful, his insights poignant.

There's something about Ahaan that resonates with me on a level I hadn't expected. It's not just his kindness or his talent, but the way he carries himself, the way he sees the world. He's a blend of strength and vulnerability, of humor and seriousness, that is incredibly appealing. Today, I saw a side of him that is thoughtful, generous, and deeply human. It's as if he's peeled back the layers to reveal a soul that is both scarred and beautiful.

As I write this, I realize that today has been more than just a series of events. It's been a journey of discovery, of seeing someone in a new light, and of allowing myself to be seen. Ahaan has shown me that sometimes, the unexpected moments, the unplanned encounters, can lead to the most meaningful connections. He's reminded me that beneath the surface of every person lies a story waiting to be told, a heart waiting to be understood.

So here I am, at the end of a day that has been as enlightening as it has been surprising, feeling a sense of warmth and anticipation for what lies ahead. Whatever the future holds, I'm grateful for this day and for the chance to see the world through Ahaan's eyes, even if just for a little while.

With a heart full of newfound wonder,
Aliza
Varanasi.

7 - Love Is In The Air

Nadeem groaned, burying his face deeper into the pillow. The thought of waking up early once again was unbearable. He longed for more sleep, his body heavy with the remnants of dreams. The hotel room, dimly lit by the early morning sun filtering through the curtains, was a cocoon of comfort he didn't want to leave.

On the other side of the room, Aliza lay wide awake. Sleep had eluded her, and the walls of the hotel room seemed to close in around her. She felt restless, yearning to embrace the freshness of the morning outside. Her thoughts wandered to Ahaan, and she wondered what he was up to at this hour.

As if on cue, her phone buzzed, breaking the silence. She reached for it and saw a message from an unknown number. Her heart skipped a beat as she opened it. The message was from Ahaan. How had he gotten her number? She quickly deduced that it must have been Nadeem. Despite her initial annoyance, she reminded herself that her brother was just a teenager, oblivious to the nuances of privacy and boundaries.

The message read: "I am having coffee at a nearby coffee shop and feeling very awkward to stare at unknown faces around me. Would you like to join?" Aliza pondered for a moment, the invitation intriguing her. She glanced at Nadeem, who was still fast asleep, snoring softly. He wouldn't wake up for another couple of hours at least.

Her decision made, Aliza quietly slipped out of bed and find a piece of paper. She scribbled a note for Nadeem, explaining where she had gone and that she would be back soon. She placed the note gently on the bedside table, making sure it was in plain sight for when he eventually woke up.

Aliza took one last look at her sleeping brother, his face peaceful and undisturbed. She grabbed her jacket and silently left the hotel room, the door clicking softly behind her. The hallway was quiet, and she could hear her own footsteps as she made her way to the elevator.

As she stepped outside, the cool morning air greeted her, invigorating her senses. The city was beginning to stir, with people bustling about, starting their day. Aliza felt a sense of excitement and anticipation as she walked towards the coffee shop. She wondered what the day would bring, and a smile tugged at her lips at the thought of seeing Ahaan again.

Aliza navigated through the narrow, winding streets, each turn bringing her closer to the address Ahaan had sent. The morning air was clear, and the city was slowly coming to life. The path was lined with charming little shops and old buildings, their facades weathered yet full of character. She felt a sense of adventure as she made her way through the maze of alleys.

Finally, she arrived at the coffee shop. It was a quaint, inviting place with large windows that allowed the morning light to flood in, casting a warm glow on the rustic wooden interior. As she approached, the first thing she noticed was Ahaan. He was sitting at a corner table, his presence striking against the backdrop of the cozy café.

Ahaan looked effortlessly handsome. He wore a navy-blue blazer over a branded white shirt, the top button casually undone. His dark jeans were perfectly tailored, and a pair of classic brown leather shoes completed his look. His hair, a rich shade of black, was neatly styled yet had a slightly tousled appearance that added to his charm. As he looked up and saw her, his deep, expressive eyes lit up with a warm smile that made her heart flutter.

Aliza couldn't help but take a moment to admire him. There was an air of confidence and ease about him that was incredibly appealing. She walked over to his table, her own smile spreading across her face as she sat down.

"You know a lot about this place," she said, her eyes glancing around the charming café. "I hope the coffee is as good as the location of this shop."

Ahaan chuckled softly, a sound that was both comforting and delightful. "I certainly hope so," he replied, his voice smooth and inviting. "This is one of my favorite spots in the city. The coffee here is excellent, and the atmosphere is perfect for a quiet morning."

Aliza felt a sense of ease wash over her. The ambiance of the café, combined with Ahaan's warm presence, made her feel at home. She sipped her coffee, savoring the rich flavor, before speaking.

"When we first met, you were wearing hippy-like clothes, and now you have such a classy look. Why the change?" she asked, curiosity in her voice.

Ahaan raised an eyebrow, a playful smirk tugging at his lips. "You're keeping a good eye on me, huh? Noticing what I wear and all?" he teased – "Are you like checking me out?"

Aliza chuckled, feeling a slight blush rise to her cheeks. "I'm just—"

Ahaan cut her off gently, his tone warm and encouraging. "No need to be formal now. Actually, today I'm meeting some sponsors in the city. They're organizing a college fest, and I want them to invite me as a guest poet."

"That's great! Can I help?" Aliza offered, her eyes sparkling with genuine interest.

Ahaan shook his head, his expression softening. "No need. If they meet you, they'll invite you as a guest author because you're such a big personality as a bestselling author, and they'll totally ignore me. I don't want that."

Aliza smiled, understanding his point. "I see. You want to shine on your own. I respect that."

Ahaan nodded, his eyes meeting hers with gratitude. "Exactly. I want to earn this opportunity on my own merits."

The conversation flowed seamlessly as they continued to share their aspirations and experiences. Aliza felt a deep connection with Ahaan, appreciating his determination and passion. For a moment, there was a comfortable silence, each lost in their thoughts, sipping their coffee.

Ahaan broke the silence, his voice gentle. "You didn't tell me about your parents."

Aliza's smile faltered slightly, and she looked down at her cup, tracing the rim with her finger. "They both died in a car accident when I was young," she began, her voice soft but steady. "I wasn't very close to them as a child. They were always busy, caught up in their own worlds. Sometimes, I feel like I don't even have any real memories of them."

She paused, gathering her thoughts. Ahaan listened intently, his eyes never leaving her face, providing silent support.

"I remember little things," Aliza continued, her gaze distant. "The sound of my mother's laugh when she was talking on the phone, the smell of my father's clothes when he hugged me goodbye in the mornings. But those are just fragments, not the whole picture. It's like trying to piece together a puzzle with most of the pieces missing."

Ahaan nodded, his expression compassionate but he didn't interrupt, allowing her to share at her own pace.

"I guess that's why I'm so close to Nadeem," she said, a hint of a smile returning to her lips. "He's my only family now. We've always looked out for each other, especially after our parents died. It was hard, but we managed. I had to grow up quickly, take care of things, and make sure Nadeem had as normal a childhood as possible."

She sighed, a mix of sadness and relief washing over her. "Sometimes, I wonder what life would have been like if they were still here. Would things be different? Would I be different? But then, I remind myself that everything that happened made me who I am today. I found strength I didn't know I had, and I learned to cherish the people who are still here."

Aliza paused, a memory surfacing. "I remember this one time," she began, her voice steady, "when I went to a parent-teacher meeting at Nadeem's school. He was in the fourth grade, and it was my first time attending such a meeting alone."

She could still recall the way the school smelled of chalk and fresh paper, the buzz of children's laughter echoing down the hallways. As she entered the classroom, the teacher, Mrs. Patel, greeted her with a warm smile, but there was a hint of curiosity in her eyes.

"We were sitting in those tiny chairs, talking about Nadeem's progress," Aliza continued. "The teachers were very impressed with his work but kept glancing at me, probably wondering where our parents were. Eventually, one of them gently asked if our parents would be joining us."

Aliza paused; the memory vivid in her mind. "I told them that our parents had passed away in a car accident. The room went silent, and I could see the sympathy and sadness in their eyes. They all felt so broken for us, but I quickly told them, 'No need to be sorry. Nadeem and I are a team, and we have both our parents inside us.'"

Ahaan listened intently, his gaze never wavering. Aliza's voice grew firmer as she continued. "Since that day, I decided I would be both a father and a mother to Nadeem. I had to. I wanted to give him all the love and support he deserved, to fill the void left by our parents. I wanted him to feel whole, even in their absence."

She took a deep breath, feeling a sense of pride in her words. "It hasn't always been easy, but Nadeem and I have a bond that's unbreakable. We've faced challenges together, and we've come out stronger on the other side. I think our parents would be proud of us."

They sat in silence for a moment, the bond between them growing stronger. Aliza felt a sense of peace, knowing she had shared a part of her life that had shaped her into the person she was today. As she looked into Ahaan's eyes, she felt a connection that went beyond words, a mutual understanding that spoke volumes.

Ahaan sought permission to touch her hand. Aliza was surprised and thought "what a gentleman he is "she nodded in acceptance. Ahaan reached across the table, giving her hand a reassuring squeeze. Aliza looked up, meeting his eyes. She felt a warmth in his gaze, a silent understanding that words couldn't capture.

"Thank you for listening," she said softly. "It feels good to talk about it."

Ahaan smiled, still holding her hand. "Anytime, Aliza."

The café around them was bustling with activity. The aroma of freshly brewed coffee mingled with the soft chatter of patrons and the gentle clinking of cups and saucers. The morning light streamed through the large windows, casting a warm, golden hue across the wooden tables and cozy chairs. The walls were adorned with vintage posters and shelves filled with books, creating an inviting and homely atmosphere.

Just then, the barista arrived with their coffee, placing the steaming cups in front of them with a friendly smile. Aliza took a moment to savor the rich aroma before taking a sip, feeling the warmth spread through her.

"Now, it's your turn," she said, leaning back in her chair. "Tell me more about your parents."

Ahaan looked thoughtful for a moment. "There's not much more to tell," he began, his voice steady but distant. "As I told you, my father died in the Kargil War. He was a brave man, and I'm proud of his sacrifice. My mother... she's devoted her life to social work, helping those in need. She's always been passionate about making a difference."

As he spoke, Aliza noticed Ahaan's gaze drifting towards a girl sitting across from them. The girl appeared pregnant and was sitting with her husband, both enjoying their coffee. Ahaan's expression grew a little uncomfortable, his eyes lingering on the couple.

Aliza followed his gaze and then looked back at Ahaan; curiosity piqued. "Is everything okay?" she asked gently.

Ahaan seemed to snap back to the present, forcing a smile. "Yeah, everything's fine. Just... thinking."

Aliza raised an eyebrow, sensing there was more to it. "Do you know them?"

Ahaan shook his head. "No, it's not that. It's just..." he paused for a moment. The uncomfortable aura of Ahaan was quite evident. He was sweating heavily. He took his handkerchief and swept all the sweat beats away and put up a smile on his face and continued, "seeing them reminds me of what I missed growing up. My parents never had the chance to share moments like that. My father was always away, and my mother was consumed by her work. I sometimes wonder what it would have been like to have a normal family, to have parents who were present."

Aliza reached across the table, placing her hand on Ahaan's. "I understand. It's hard to miss out on those things. But you've turned out to be an amazing person despite it all." But something was off. Aliza realized that something was not right, but she couldn't put a finger on it. Did Ahaan know the girl and something just clicked or something came up that shook him because she had never seen Ahaan doing such a thing before. For a while she just tried to ignore everything and put up a smile on her face.

The café continued to buzz around them, but for a moment, it felt like they were in their own world, sharing a connection that went beyond words. Aliza felt a deep empathy for Ahaan, understanding his struggles and the pain of his past. They sat in companionable silence for a while, each lost in their thoughts, the coffee between them growing cold. Soon the pregnant lady and the man who sat with her left the coffee shop and Aliza saw a sudden relief in Ahaan's eyes.

Eventually, Ahaan took a deep breath, his expression clearing. "You know, despite everything, I wouldn't change my past. It made me who I am today, and I've met some incredible people along the way."

Aliza smiled, feeling a renewed sense of connection with Ahaan. "I feel the same way. Our pasts shape us, but they don't define us. It's the choices we make and the people we meet that really matter."

Ahaan nodded, his eyes shining with appreciation. "Here's to new beginnings and the journey ahead."

They clinked their coffee cups together, sealing their shared understanding and the promise of future adventures. The morning was still young, and as they finished their coffee, both Aliza and Ahaan felt a sense of excitement and anticipation for what lay ahead.

Suddenly, Aliza's phone buzzed. She glanced at the screen and saw Nadeem's name flashing. Answering the call, she heard his voice, sounding slightly anxious.

"Where are you?" Nadeem asked.

"I left a note for you. Can't you read?" Aliza replied, trying to keep her tone light. She was not expecting Nadeem's call because for a while she forgot about the rest of the world completely.

"Come back, I'm not feeling good," Nadeem said, his voice wavering slightly. Nadeem said nothing after that and paused. He kept the call running and after that the call was cut.

Alarmed, Aliza exchanged a worried glance with Ahaan. "We need to go," she said, hastily grabbing her bag. Ahaan had no idea what happened but read the expressions of Aliza and knew it was something alarming and they both had to respond quick.

They quickly left the café and hurried back to the hotel, the bustling streets a blur around them. The concern for Nadeem's well-being propelled them forward, and they reached the hotel in record time. Rushing up to the room, Aliza fumbled with the key card before finally opening the door.

Inside, they found Nadeem lying on his bed, his face pale. Aliza rushed to his side, her heart pounding. "What happened?" she asked, her voice full of worry. She kept her palm on the forehead of Nadeem to check whether he had fever or something.

Nadeem moaned and shifted slightly. "I kept sleeping and

skipped breakfast, and now I'm hungry," he mumbled, his eyes barely open.

Aliza's worry quickly turned to fury. She felt strange for a while and then said, "You said you weren't feeling well! I thought you were seriously ill or something!"

Nadeem managed a weak smile, his attempt at humor evident. "I am not feeling well. I'm hungry."

Despite her anger, Aliza couldn't help but roll her eyes at his strange sense of humor. "You scared me half to death, Nadeem! Next time, just say you're hungry."

Nadeem's smile widened as he let out a soft laugh. "Sorry, sis and oh! Good morning stranger." He said to Ahaan.

Before Ahaan could reply his phone buzzed with a call. He glanced at the screen and saw it was from the place where he had a meeting scheduled. Excusing himself, he answered the call, stepping out of the room for a moment.

Aliza sighed, her anger dissipating as she ruffled Nadeem's hair affectionately. "Alright, let's get you something to eat. You really know how to worry me, you know that?"

Nadeem nodded, his stomach growling loudly. "I know. Sorry, Aliza."

Ahaan returned, looking slightly preoccupied. "I have to go," he said, his tone apologetic. "The meeting is about to start, and I need to be there on time."

Aliza nodded, understanding. "Good luck, Ahaan. And thank you for coming with me."

Ahaan smiled warmly. "Anytime, Aliza. I hope Nadeem feels

better soon." Nadeem and Ahaan smirked.

With a final wave, Ahaan left the room, leaving Aliza and Nadeem alone. Aliza turned her attention back to her brother, her expression softening. "Let's get you some breakfast, okay?"

Nadeem nodded eagerly. "Yes, please."

They ordered room service, and soon a tray laden with food arrived. As Nadeem ate swiftly, Aliza watched him with a mixture of relief and affection. Despite the scare, she felt grateful for moments like these, where their bond was reaffirmed.

As Nadeem polished off his breakfast, he looked up at Aliza, his eyes full of gratitude. "Thanks, sis."

Aliza smiled, her heart swelling with love for her brother. "Anytime, Nadeem. Just promise me you'll be more clear next time."

Nadeem laughed; his earlier discomfort forgotten. "I promise."

The room filled with laughter and the clinking of cutlery, the earlier tension melting away. Aliza knew that no matter what challenges lay ahead, she and Nadeem would face them together, just as they always had.

8 - The Wedding Invitation

After ensuring that Nadeem was comfortably resting and well-fed, Aliza decided to catch up on some work. She opened her laptop and began going through the messages on her social media accounts. As a popular writer, staying connected with her fans was essential. She valued their support and took the time to reply to as many messages as possible.

The first message she came across was from a fan named Priya:
Priya: "Hi Aliza! I just finished reading your latest book and I couldn't put it down. Your writing is so inspiring! Thank you for sharing your stories with us."

Aliza: "Thank you so much, Priya! I'm thrilled to hear that you enjoyed my book. Your support means the world to me. Keep reading and stay inspired!"

The next message was from a young aspiring writer named Rahul:
Rahul: "Hi Aliza, I'm an aspiring writer and I wanted to ask if you have any tips for someone just starting out?"

Aliza: "Hi Rahul! The best advice I can give is to write every day, no matter how much or how little. Don't be afraid to make mistakes and always be open to learning and improving. Good luck with your writing journey!"

As she continued to respond to messages, she came across one that made her heart skip a beat. It was from a long-lost friend, Ananya: **Ananya:** "Are you seriously in Varanasi? How can you not think about me? I am in the city as well. Come and meet me, here's my number."

Aliza stared at the message, memories of their childhood friendship flooding back. She hadn't seen or spoken to Ananya in years. Without hesitating, she decided to call her friend. She quickly dialed the number and waited, her heart pounding with anticipation.

"Hello?" came a familiar voice on the other end of the line.

"Ananya? It's Aliza!" she exclaimed, unable to hide her excitement.

"Aliza! Oh my God, I can't believe it's you!" Ananya replied, her voice filled with joy. "How have you been? It's been ages!"

"I know, it's been too long," Aliza agreed. "I can't believe we're both in Varanasi at the same time. What a coincidence!"

"It's amazing! We have so much to catch up on," Ananya said. "How are you? What brings you to Varanasi?"

"I'm here with my brother, Nadeem. We're taking a short break and exploring the city," Aliza explained. "How about you? What have you been up to?"

"I'm here for my sister's wedding, which is in two days in Allahabad," Ananya said. "I would love for you to come. It would be so great to have you there!"

Aliza hesitated for a moment, considering the invitation. It had been a long time since she had attended a wedding, and the chance to reconnect with Ananya was too good to pass up. "I'd love to come," she said finally. "It would be wonderful to see you and celebrate your sister's wedding."

"Fantastic!" Ananya exclaimed. "I'll send you all the details. I can't wait to see you again, Aliza. We have so much to talk about."

"Me too, Ananya. I'm really looking forward to it," Aliza replied, feeling a rush of excitement.

They chatted for a few more minutes, catching up on old times and reminiscing about their shared memories. When the call finally ended, Aliza felt a sense of happiness and nostalgia. She was eager to reunite with her friend and to be part of such a special occasion.

As she closed her laptop, Aliza couldn't help but smile. Life had a funny way of bringing people back together, and she was grateful for the opportunity to reconnect with Ananya. The upcoming wedding in Allahabad promised to be a joyous event, and Aliza was ready to embrace the new memories that awaited her.

After responding to a few more messages, Aliza felt exhaustion creeping in. She leaned back in her chair, closing her eyes for a moment. The weight of everything started to settle on her shoulders. She had come to Varanasi to find inspiration for her next novel, but so far, she hadn't found a concrete plot. Her mind wandered back to her conversation with Ahaan and the events of the past few days.

"Wait a minute," she thought, a spark of realization igniting in her mind. "Maybe I do have a plot. I have a whole story to share. My own story."

The idea seemed both daunting and exhilarating. She thought about the challenges and triumphs she had faced, the bond she shared with Nadeem, and her budding connection with Ahaan. Was it too early to call it a story? Could she weave the elements of her life into a narrative that would resonate with readers?

Her mind began to race with possibilities. "Ahaan and Aliza," she mused. "It sounds good."

Aliza grabbed a notebook and pen, starting to jot down ideas. She wrote about the loss of her parents, the responsibilities she had taken on at a young age, and the unbreakable bond she shared with Nadeem. She noted her serendipitous meeting with Ahaan, their deepening connection, and the way he had opened up to her about his own struggles and aspirations.

As she wrote, a story began to take shape. It was a tale of resilience, love, and the power of human connections. It was a story of two people finding solace and strength in each other while navigating the complexities of their pasts.

She paused, her pen hovering over the page. Could she really turn her personal experiences into a novel? Would people be interested in reading about her life? The doubts crept in, but Aliza pushed them aside. This story was worth telling, and she was the only one who could tell it.

Feeling a renewed sense of purpose, Aliza continued to write, fleshing out the characters and their journeys. She envisioned scenes and dialogues, drawing from her own emotions and experiences. The more she wrote, the more confident she felt that this was the story she was meant to share.

Hours passed, and the exhaustion she had felt earlier was replaced by a sense of excitement and determination. She was so absorbed in her writing that she didn't notice the time slipping away. It was only when Nadeem stirred in his bed, stretching and yawning, that she looked up from her notebook.

"Hey, sis," Nadeem said, rubbing his eyes. "What are you doing?"

Aliza smiled, closing her notebook. "Just working on my next novel. I think I finally found the plot."

Nadeem smiled, looking genuinely interested. "Really? What's it about?"

"It's about us," Aliza replied, her eyes sparkling with enthusiasm. "It's about our journey, the challenges we've faced, and the people we've met along the way. It's about finding strength in each other and the power of human connections."

Nadeem's smile widened. "Isn't it too dramatic?"

"Maybe but few people like to read drama as well." Aliza replied.

"Am I the main character? I want to be a main character in the novel and do describe me as the most handsome guy on earth. I want your readers to ask for my phone number, especially pretty girls." Nadeem was serious when he said so.

"Will do my best," Aliza said, with a hint of smile on her face. "I think it's going to be something special."

Just then, her phone buzzed again. This time, it was a message from Ananya, sharing the details of her sister's wedding. Aliza read the message and smiled. It was yet another chapter in the story she was writing, both in her novel and in her life.

As she looked out the window at the bustling city of Varanasi, Aliza felt a sense of peace. She was exactly where she needed to be, surrounded by the people who mattered most. And with that thought, she knew that the story she was about to tell would be a reflection of her heart and soul, capturing the essence of her journey in a way that would resonate with readers everywhere.

It was late at night, and Aliza found herself glancing at her phone more frequently than she would like to admit. The absence of any message or call from Ahaan was gnawing at her, making her increasingly impatient. She wanted him to reach out, to hear his voice and know how his meeting had gone. The anticipation was driving her mad, but she couldn't bring herself to make the first move.

Dinner time arrived, and Aliza and Nadeem headed out to a nearby restaurant. The ambiance was cozy, with soft lighting and the hum of conversations blending with the clinking of cutlery. They settled into their seats, and Nadeem immediately dived into the menu, trying to decide what to order.

Aliza, however, couldn't focus. Her mind was still preoccupied with Ahaan. As they waited for their food, she finally gave in and called him, unable to bear the suspense any longer.

The phone rang a few times before Ahaan picked up. "Hello?" His voice sounded subdued, lacking its usual warmth.

"Hey, Ahaan," Aliza said, trying to keep her tone light. "I was just checking in. How did your meeting go?"

There was a pause before Ahaan responded. "It didn't go well," he admitted, his voice heavy with disappointment. "The sponsors weren't interested. They said my work wasn't what they were looking for. It was... disheartening, to say the least."

Aliza's heart sank at the sadness in his voice. She struggled to find the right words, unsure of how to cheer him up. "I'm so sorry to hear that, Ahaan. I know how much this meant to you."

"It's okay," he replied, though it was clear he was trying to mask his disappointment. "I'll keep trying. It's just one setback, right?"

"Absolutely," Aliza said, wishing she could do more to comfort him. "You're incredibly talented, Ahaan. Don't let this one experience bring you down. There will be other opportunities."

"Thanks, Aliza," Ahaan said softly. "Can I call you later? I am feeling sleepy. Will talk to you later." He said and cut the call.

Their food arrived, and they tried to focus on their meal, but Aliza's thoughts kept drifting back to Ahaan. She couldn't shake the feeling of wanting to do something more, to help him see the light at the end of this dark tunnel.

"Do you want to meet him?" Nadeem asked, his voice gentle but firm. "I can't see you like this. I need to eat and I want you to be happy as well."

There was a long silence. Aliza looked at her brother, feeling torn. The concern in his eyes mirrored her own. She knew he was right; she couldn't shake off the worry for Ahaan, and it was affecting both of them.

After what felt like an eternity, Nadeem asked for the waiter.

The waiter arrived a few minutes later and said, "Yes sir, how can I help you?"

Nadeem, taking charge, said, "Can you please pack all this for us? We'll go to our hotel and then eat this. I am not feeling quite good at the moment."

"Yes sir, sure." The waiter quickly took all the food and packed it, returning shortly with the packets.

As they prepared to leave, Nadeem looked at Aliza with a determined expression. "Ahaan's on the third floor of our hotel. I know his room number. Let's go see him."

Aliza nodded, grateful for Nadeem's initiative. They left the restaurant and made their way back to the hotel. The night air was cool and refreshing, a stark contrast to the tension Aliza felt inside.

When they arrived at the hotel, they took the elevator to the third floor. Nadeem led the way, navigating the corridors until they reached Ahaan's room. He knocked on the door gently, but with purpose.

There was a moment of silence before they heard footsteps approaching. The door opened, and Ahaan stood there, looking surprised and a bit disheveled. His eyes widened when he saw Aliza and Nadeem standing there with their packed dinner.

"Hey," Ahaan said, his voice soft. "What are you guys doing here?"

Aliza stepped forward; her concern evident. "We couldn't just leave you alone after what happened. Nadeem suggested we come and have dinner together."

Ahaan's expression softened, a mix of gratitude and relief washing over him. "You didn't have to do that, but... thank you. I appreciate it."

"Of course we did," Aliza said, her voice firm but warm. "We're friends, right? We're here for each other. Nadeem teasingly said, "Just friends or something else ha?" to which Aliza replied "Shut up".

Ahaan stepped aside, letting them in. The room was simple but comfortable, with a small sitting area by the window. They settled down, unpacking the food and spreading it out on the coffee table. The room's warm lighting and the scent of their dinner created a cozy, intimate atmosphere.

As they began to eat, the atmosphere gradually lightened. Nadeem, ever the icebreaker, started sharing funny anecdotes from their childhood, making both Aliza and Ahaan laugh. The tension that had been weighing them down started to lift, replaced by a sense of fellowship.

"Remember the time we tried to bake a cake for my friend's birthday, and it turned into a disaster?" Nadeem said, grinning.

Aliza chuckled. "Oh, yes! The cake was so burnt we had to throw it away, but we managed to make your friend laugh about it. He loved our effort more than anything."

Ahaan smiled, listening intently. "Sounds like you two have always had each other's backs."

"We have," Nadeem said, his voice earnest. "And now we've got yours too, Ahaan."

Ahaan's eyes shimmered with gratitude. "I don't know what to say. It's been a rough day and having you both here... it means a lot."

Aliza reached out and placed a comforting hand on Ahaan's arm. "We're here for you, Ahaan. Everyone has bad days, but you're not alone. We'll get through this together."

They continued to eat and chat, the conversation flowing easily. Aliza noticed that Ahaan was slowly starting to relax, his posture less tense, and his smiles more genuine. The disheartening experience from the meeting was still there, but it no longer seemed to weigh him down as heavily.

After they finished their meal, Nadeem excused himself to the bathroom, leaving Aliza and Ahaan alone. There was a comfortable silence between them as they tidied up the food containers.

Ahaan looked at Aliza, his expression thoughtful. "You know, I was feeling so defeated after the meeting today. I really needed this—needed you. Thank you for being here."

Aliza smiled warmly. "Anytime, Ahaan. You've been there for me too. We're a team now, remember?"

Ahaan's eyes softened. "Yeah, we are. And I'm glad."

There was a silence for a while, and then Nadeem, ever the lively spirit, piped up, "Two of the members of this team are now going to Allahabad. Would the third member like to join?"

Ahaan looked hesitant. "I don't know, guys. I have some work and all…"

Aliza gave him a knowing look. "Now you're doing the same thing I was doing earlier, Ahaan. I know you have nothing pressing, and besides, you want to know me better, and I want to know you. What better way to do that than by going to an Indian wedding together?"

Ahaan chuckled, trying to maintain his reluctance. "I don't want to intrude or anything…"

Nadeem jumped in with a mischievous grin. "Intrude? Dude, Indian weddings are all about people showing up, even if they're barely related or not at all! Plus, who doesn't want to experience the chaos and fun of an Indian wedding? Trust me, you'll love it. And how can you ignore the girls?"

Ahaan and Aliza both looked at Nadeem. Nadeem simply smiled.

Ahaan still seemed unsure, so Aliza added, "Come on, Ahaan. It'll be fun. We'll get to celebrate, dance, eat amazing food, and you'll get to see a different side of the Indian culture. Besides, I could use some moral support, and Nadeem could use another person to pester."

Nadeem chuckled widely. "Yeah, Ahaan, you'll be my accomplice. We can team up against Aliza and tease her about all the wedding stuff. Plus, who knows? Maybe you'll get some poetic inspiration for your next work."

Ahaan laughed, feeling the warmth and sincerity in their words. He realized how much he needed a break, something to lift his spirits and distract him from the disappointment of the day.

"Alright, alright. You've convinced me. I'll come with you to Allahabad."

Nadeem cheered, "Yes! This is going to be epic. Ahaan, prepare yourself for a lot of eating and enjoying!"

Aliza smiled, feeling a sense of satisfaction and excitement. "Great! It's settled then. We'll all go together. It's going to be a memorable trip."

Ahaan nodded, a smile spreading across his face. "I'm looking forward to it. Thanks, guys. I really appreciate this."

Nadeem clapped his hands together. "Alright, team! Let's get ready for the adventure of a lifetime. Allahabad, here we come!"

The three of them laughed, the room filled with a renewed sense of affinity and anticipation. The upcoming wedding trip was exactly what they all needed—a chance to bond, to celebrate, and to create new memories together. As they began to plan the details of their journey, the excitement grew, and Aliza couldn't help but feel grateful for the unexpected twists and turns that had brought them all together.

Dear Diary # 1

Dear Diary,

What a day it has been, and as I sit here under the soft glow of the hotel lamp, I feel a mixture of exhaustion and exhilaration. Today unfolded in ways I couldn't have predicted, and it's left me with so much to ponder.

The day began with an unexpected surprise—an invitation to an old friend's sister's wedding in Allahabad. The message brought back a flood of memories, reminding me of a simpler time when friendships were less complicated and life felt a bit more predictable. But before I could fully process this, the day took another turn.

Nadeem and I had decided to head out for dinner, but my mind was preoccupied. I hadn't heard from Ahaan all day, and it was gnawing at me. It's strange how quickly someone can become a fixture in your thoughts. The anticipation of his call made me restless, and finally, I gave in and called him.

When Ahaan picked up, I could hear the weariness in his voice. His meeting hadn't gone well, and he was clearly disheartened. We talked briefly, and I could sense his reluctance to share the depth of his disappointment. That feeling of helplessness washed over me, and I wished I could do more to lift his spirits.

When Nadeem and I decided to bump in his room, I was excited. Ahaan opened the door, the surprise on his face quickly melted into gratitude. Seeing him standing there, disheveled yet relieved, stirred something in me. The three of us settled in his room, spreading out our packed dinner on the small coffee table. The room, though simple, felt warmer with our presence.

We ate, and Nadeem, in his usual fashion, lightened the mood with childhood stories. The laughter was like a balm, soothing the day's rough edges. Ahaan gradually relaxed, his posture less tense, his smiles more genuine. The burden of his disappointing meeting seemed to lift, if only for a while.

After dinner, Nadeem, ever the instigator of adventures, mentioned the upcoming wedding in Allahabad. His suggestion that Ahaan join us was met with hesitation. Ahaan tried to beg off, mentioning work, but I saw through his excuse. He was doing exactly what I had done earlier—building walls to protect himself.

I called him out on it, encouraging him to join us, to let go of his worries, and to embrace the spontaneity of the moment. Nadeem, with his usual humor, emphasized the joys of an Indian wedding, promising an experience Ahaan wouldn't want to miss. Reluctantly, Ahaan agreed, and I felt a surge of triumph and relief.

As we returned to our room, the sense of togetherness and anticipation was palpable. Nadeem's excitement was infectious, and Ahaan's presence felt like a promise of new memories waiting to be made. The idea of attending the wedding together added a new dimension to our unfolding story, and I couldn't wait to see where it would lead.

Tonight, after Nadeem had fallen asleep, I found myself reflecting on the day's events. Ahaan's vulnerability, his willingness to join us, and the growing bond between us all made me realize how much our lives had intertwined. There was something profoundly comforting about the way we had come together, each bringing our own strengths and flaws to the table.

As I prepare for bed, I'm filled with a sense of excitement and curiosity. The journey to Allahabad promises to be an adventure, not just for the wedding festivities but for the deeper connections we are forging. Ahaan's presence adds a layer of unpredictability, a reminder that life's best moments often come unplanned.

So here I am, at the end of another extraordinary day, feeling grateful for the twists and turns that have brought us here. The future feels wide open, filled with possibilities and the promise of new beginnings. I can't wait to see what tomorrow brings, knowing that whatever it is, we'll face it together.

Oh! And how did I forget to tell you? I have started writing the book as well. My new book about my own life and maybe the beginning of a life with someone special. Who knows where the life has planned to take us. I am all in for the adventure.

With a heart brimming with anticipation,
Aliza
Varanasi.

9 - The Strange Encounter

Nadeem, Aliza, and Ahaan finally started their journey to Allahabad, the anticipation of the wedding making the air feel electric. They booked a taxi, an SUV that promised a comfortable ride for the three-hour journey ahead. As they settled into the plush seats, the cityscape of Varanasi gradually gave way to the open, sprawling countryside. The road stretched ahead like a ribbon of possibilities, flanked by fields of green and golden hues that seemed to stretch into eternity.

The journey was anything but dull. Nadeem, the eternal source of entertainment, kept the conversation lively with his anecdotes and light-hearted banter. Aliza occasionally chimed in with her own stories, while Ahaan, still somewhat reserved, began to open up more as the kilometers ticked by. They shared laughter followed by a few quiet moments of introspection, each of them lost in their own thoughts but comforted by the presence of the others.

As they neared Allahabad, the landscape started to change. The roads became busier, the air richer with the scents of local cuisine wafting from roadside stalls, and the excitement of the approaching celebration palpable. The taxi finally pulled up to the venue, and the sight that greeted them was nothing short of breathtaking.

The wedding venue was a grandiose mansion, its architecture a blend of traditional Indian and contemporary styles. The main gate was adorned with a massive floral archway, resplendent with marigolds, roses, and jasmine, their fragrances mingling to create an intoxicating scent. Strings of fairy lights were draped artistically across the entire facade, twinkling like stars in the evening light.

As they entered through the archway, the expanse of the front lawn opened up before them. It was a scene straight out of a fairytale. The lawn was dotted with elegant canopies in vibrant colors, each one housing beautifully decorated seating arrangements. Guests dressed in their finest attire milled about, their laughter and conversations blending into a harmonious hum.

In the center of the lawn stood the gazebo, the sacred wedding pavilion. It was an elaborate structure, adorned with golden drapes and intricate floral arrangements. The pillars were wrapped in garlands of white lilies and red roses, and crystal chandeliers hung from the canopy, casting a soft, romantic glow over the entire setup.

To the side, a grand stage was set for the evening's entertainment. The decorations were still going on around them. The buffet area was a culinary paradise, with an array of dishes from various regions of India, each one more tempting than the last. Chefs in white coats moved efficiently, ensuring that every detail was perfect.

Nadeem's eyes widened with awe as he took in the scene. "Wow, this is incredible! Is she really your friend? How come you became friend with such a wealthy girl?" he exclaimed; his excitement infectious.

Aliza nodded, her gaze sweeping over the magnificence of the setup. "Even I had no clue that she was such wealthy? She used to quarrel me over a 12 Rupees patty back in those days," she murmured, feeling a sense of magic in the air. She said with all her serious expressions on.

Ahaan, standing beside her, looked equally impressed. "Indian weddings are something else, and people always end up spending more than they should" he said, a smile playing on his lips. "I'm glad I decided to come. I am sure I'll get some hot chicks here." It was a soft banter from Ahaan. Aliza knew but still showed her big eyes to him.

They made their way further into the crowd, greeted by the vibrant sounds of the crowd in the background. Everywhere they looked, there were splashes of color and intricate designs—from the richly embroidered saris and sherwanis worn by the guests to the elaborate henna patterns adorning the hands of the women. For a time being, all three of them felt they were under dressed for the occasion and were clearly looking odd ones out.

Ahaan couldn't help but be captivated by the sheer spectacle of it all. The warm, welcoming atmosphere, the richness of the traditions, and the joyous energy of the guests were unlike anything he had experienced before. He felt a sense of belonging, a connection to this world that was both new and enchanting.

As they mingled with the other guests, Aliza spotted her old friend who had invited them. Ananya waved enthusiastically from a distance and hurried over, embracing Aliza warmly.

"I'm so glad you made it!" Ananya exclaimed, her eyes sparkling with excitement. "And you brought company!"

"I hope I'm not crashing the wedding here," Ahaan said, extending his hand for a handshake.

Ananya shook his hand with a smile. "We've invited 500 guests, but the food is for 600, so we have plenty of space for handsome guys like you."

They all smiled, but Aliza felt somewhat protective of Ahaan and quickly switched the topic. "Where are the other girls and the bride?" she asked.

Ananya chuckled, understanding Aliza's subtle deflection. "Oh, they're all in the bridal suite, getting ready. You know how it is— lots of last-minute touch-ups and nerves."

Aliza nodded, glancing around the lively scene. "I'd love to say hi to them before the ceremony starts."

"Of course! Come with me," Ananya said, looping her arm through Aliza's. "Ahaan and Nadeem, feel free to explore or grab some food. We'll be back soon."

As Ananya and Aliza made their way towards the bridal suite, Ahaan and Nadeem looked at each other, shrugged, and decided to head to the buffet area.

"You know, I think Ananya likes you," Nadeem teased, nudging Ahaan with his elbow.

Ahaan laughed, shaking his head. "I know. Who can resist such a cute guy like me?" Ahaan teased back. "And don't worry. You'll also get someone soon."

"Huh, I don't need anyone. I already have lots of girls at school to treat me well," Nadeem said, piling food onto his plate. "And speaking of treats, this food looks amazing!"

Back in the bridal suite, Aliza was greeted with squeals of joy from her old friends. The bride, Ananya's sister Priya, was sitting in front of a mirror, looking radiant in her traditional red and gold bridal attire.

"Aliza! I'm so happy you're here," Priya said, standing up to hug her. "You look beautiful."

"Not as beautiful as you," Aliza replied, hugging her back. "How are you feeling?"

"Nervous, excited, overwhelmed—everything at once," Priya admitted, her eyes shining.

"You'll be fine," Aliza reassured her. "Just take deep breaths and enjoy every moment."

As they chatted, Aliza's phone buzzed. It was a message from Ahaan: *Just met some interesting people at the buffet. Can't wait to tell you about it. And by the way, the food is incredible!*

Aliza smiled, feeling a warm glow inside. She replied quickly: *Glad you're having fun! Save some food for me. I'll join you guys soon.*

Back in the lawn, Ahaan and Nadeem were indeed having a great time. They had joined a group of young men and women who were discussing the latest Bollywood movies and music.

"So, Ahaan, are you really a poet?" one of the girls asked, her eyes wide with curiosity.

"Yes, I am," Ahaan replied modestly. "I perform at small gigs and events. It's my passion."

"Can we hear some of your poetry here?" another guest requested, and soon the entire group was encouraging him.

Ahaan smiled, feeling a bit bashful but also thrilled by their enthusiasm. "Alright, but only if you promise to join in."

The group settled down, forming a small circle around Ahaan. He took a deep breath, closing his eyes for a moment as he gathered his thoughts. When he opened them again, he began to recite, his voice steady and resonant:

"The title is, 'in the heart of the night'…" he began reciting…

> In the heart of the night, when the world sleeps tight,
> I wander through dreams, in the soft moonlight.
> Stars whisper secrets, the breeze hums a tune,
> Lost in the wonder, under the watchful moon.
> In the heart of the night, shadows dance and play,
> They tell tales of love, in their own silent way.
> The trees sway gently, in a rhythmic embrace,

As if they remember, an old lover's face.
In the heart of the night, when time seems to slow,
I ponder on paths, where my heart longs to go.
The silence speaks volumes, of joys and of fears,
Echoes of laughter, and suppressed tears.
In the heart of the night, I find solace and peace,
A moment of stillness, where worries cease.
The world fades away, leaving only the stars,
Guiding me gently, through life's hidden scars.
In the heart of the night, dreams take their flight,
Weaving through darkness, chasing the light.
And as dawn approaches, with its soft, golden hue,
I carry the night's whispers, as morning breaks through.

The group sat in rapt silence, captivated by Ahaan's words. When he finished, there was a moment of stillness, as if everyone was absorbing the beauty of the poetry. Then, a huge applause broke out, genuine and heartfelt.

"That was beautiful," one of the girls said, her voice filled with admiration.

"Thank you," Ahaan replied, his cheeks tinged with a slight blush. "I'm glad you enjoyed it."

Aliza, who had been listening intently, felt a swell of pride for Ahaan. His poetry had a way of touching hearts, of weaving emotions into words with such grace and depth.

Nadeem, always the icebreaker, beamed and said, "Wow, Ahaan! You should perform at all the weddings. You'd steal the show every time."

Everyone laughed, and the mood lightened even further. The impromptu poetry session had brought them all closer, creating a bond that felt both new and timeless.

As the evening continued, Aliza, Ahaan, and Nadeem immersed themselves in the festivities, sharing laughter and stories and enjoying the delicious food. The grand wedding in Allahabad had become more than just a celebration of love; it was a celebration of friendship and the beautiful connections that life often unexpectedly brings.

After the initial introductions, banter, and merriment, the main ceremony began. The bride and groom, resplendent in their traditional attire, took their places at the center stage. The air was thick with anticipation and the sweet scent of marigolds, their petals scattered all around.

The wedding ceremony began, the hands of the Groom and the bride linked in an unbreakable bond. Aliza and Ahaan sat side by side, watching the ceremony unfold.

Aliza glanced at Ahaan, who was staring intently at the couple. She noticed the soft smile playing on his lips, the way his eyes glistened with a mix of emotions. Without realizing it, her thoughts began to drift into a dream-like state. She imagined herself and Ahaan in the same setting, taking those sacred vows, promising to be with each other through every joy and sorrow, every high and low.

In her vision, she saw herself in a beautiful red wedding attire, adorned with intricate gold embroidery. The fabric shimmered under the lights, each thread reflecting the love and commitment she felt in her heart. Her bangles chimed softly with each step, a delicate symphony that echoed the beating of her heart. Her hair was adorned with jasmine flowers, their fragrance mingling with the ambience.

Aliza's heart raced as she felt Ahaan's hand in hers, warm and reassuring. His touch sent a thrill through her, grounding her in the moment yet making her feel like she was floating. She looked up into his eyes, and they shared a look that spoke volumes, a silent conversation filled with love, hope, and dreams for the future.

They began to walk around, each step a promise, a commitment to each other and to the life they would build together. The lights danced and flickered, casting a golden glow that seemed to envelop them in a protective embrace. As they took the step towards marriage, they made vows that resonated deep within their souls.

"I promise to always support you in your dreams and ambitions," Ahaan said, his voice steady and filled with conviction. "I will be your rock, your anchor in every storm."

Aliza felt her eyes welling up with tears of joy. "I vow to be your strength, your support, and your eternal partner. Together, we will face all that life throws our way, hand in hand."

Ahaan's eyes softened, a tender smile playing on his lips. "I promise to cherish you, to make you laugh, and to wipe away your tears. You are my heart, my soul, my everything."

The petals rained down upon them from the heavens. Each petal seemed to carry a blessing, a wish for their happiness and prosperity. The soft rustle of the petals as they landed around them created a cocoon of serenity, isolating them from the rest of the world.

Their hearts beat in perfect harmony, and Aliza felt a peace and happiness she had never known. She could see their future unfolding before her eyes: a life filled with love, laughter, and shared dreams. She saw them traveling the world together, exploring new places, and making memories. She saw quiet evenings at home, their hands intertwined as they read or watched movies. She saw children, a testament to their love, growing up in a home filled with warmth and affection.

The world around them faded, leaving only the two of them, bound by love and destiny. The guests' murmurs, and the bustling activity of the wedding all became a distant hum, as if they were in a bubble where only their love existed.

Ahaan turned to her in this dream, his voice tender and full of love. "Aliza, I promise to stand by you, to cherish you, and to love you every day of our lives. You are my heart, my soul, my everything."

Aliza's eyes filled with tears of joy. "Ahaan, I vow to be your strength, your support, and your eternal partner. Together, we will face all that life throws our way, hand in hand."

The universe seemed to acknowledge their promises, the stars twinkling brighter in the night sky as if celebrating their union.

Suddenly, the dream was interrupted by a voice calling her name. "Aliza!" Her old friend Ananya's voice cut through the haze of her daydream.

"Aliza!" The voice jolted her back to reality. It was her old friend Ananya, who had come up to them with a bright smile. "Come on, the bride and groom are about to exchange garlands. You can't miss this part!"

Aliza blinked, the dreamy haze lifting. She realized she had been lost in her own world, and a blush crept up her cheeks. She glanced at Ahaan, who was now looking at her curiously.

"Everything okay?" he asked, his voice gentle.

Aliza smiled, shaking off the remnants of her daydream. "Yes, everything's fine. Let's go watch the rest of the ceremony."

As they joined the crowd, Aliza's heart was still racing. The dream lingered in her mind, a beautiful vision of what could be. She knew it was just a fantasy, but a part of her couldn't help but wonder if someday, somehow, that dream might become a reality.

Now, everyone was gathered around the stage, phones out, groups of friends hooting and cheering as the garlands were about to be exchanged. The bride and groom were laughing, their joy infectious. Close friends were teasing, making the moment even more delightful.

Aliza and Ahaan stood at a corner; their presence understated yet significant. For the first time, their hands touched. The brief contact sent a jolt through Aliza, her pulse quickening. She glanced at Ahaan, and he smiled softly, his eyes reflecting the same unspoken connection.

The atmosphere around them buzzed with excitement, but in that moment, it felt as if they were in their own bubble. Ahaan's fingers intertwined with hers, a silent promise of something deeper. They stood close, shoulders brushing, sharing the warmth of each other's presence. Aliza felt a sense of completeness, as if this was where she was meant to be.

Just then, Ananya came bustling through the crowd, her face lit up with excitement. "Aliza! There's someone you have to meet."

Aliza reluctantly let go of Ahaan's hand and turned to Ananya, who was accompanied by a heavily pregnant woman. "This is Marry, our long-lost friend!"

Aliza's mind raced as she tried to place the familiar face. Then it clicked. "Marry! Oh my gosh, it's been forever!" She embraced Marry warmly, feeling a rush of old memories flooding back.

"I know, right? I couldn't believe it when Ananya told me you were here!" Marry said, her voice filled with nostalgia.

Aliza turned to introduce Ahaan, but as she did, she noticed something strange. Ahaan's expression had changed. His face had gone pale, and he seemed to be shaking slightly.

"Ahaan, this is Marry. She's an old friend of mine," Aliza said, her voice trailing off as she saw the fear in Ahaan's eyes.

Ahaan offered a shaky smile, but it was clear he was deeply uncomfortable. Without a word, he turned and bolted from the scene, leaving Aliza and Marry standing there in stunned silence.

"What was that about?" Marry asked, looking bewildered.

"I... I don't know," Aliza stammered, feeling a knot of worry form in her stomach. She had never seen Ahaan like this. "I need to go check on him."

She gave Marry an apologetic look and hurried after Ahaan, her heart pounding. Aliza excused herself from the crowd, her mind racing with questions and concerns. As she stepped outside, the cool night air hit her, providing a momentary relief from the overwhelming atmosphere inside. She spotted Ahaan from a distance, leaning against a pillar. He was visibly shaking, his hands trembling as he ran them through his hair repeatedly.

Seeing him like this, so vulnerable and distressed, filled Aliza with a mix of worry and confusion. She had never seen Ahaan lose his composure like this. He was always the calm, collected one, the rock she could rely on. But now, he looked like a man haunted by his past, struggling to keep himself together.

She took a deep breath and walked over to him, her heart pounding in her chest. "Ahaan," she called softly, not wanting to startle him.

Ahaan looked up, his eyes wide and filled with a mix of fear and regret. His usual confident demeanor was gone, replaced by a raw vulnerability that made Aliza's heart ache. "I'm sorry, Aliza. I didn't mean to cause a scene," he said, his voice trembling.

Aliza reached out and took his hand, squeezing it gently. "You don't have to apologize. I just want to make sure you're okay. What happened back there?"

Ahaan looked away, his shoulders slumping. "Seeing Marry... it brought back a lot of memories. Memories I thought I had buried, but they all came rushing back the moment I saw her."

Aliza felt a pang of jealousy mixed with concern. "What kind of memories?" she asked, her voice gentle.

Ahaan didn't say anything, his silence speaking volumes. Aliza stood beside him, her mind racing with questions and concerns. She wondered what kind of memories Ahaan was trying to bury, what part of his past was so painful that it still haunted him. The uncertainty gnawed at her. What if there were things about Ahaan she didn't know, things that could change how she felt about him? Could she trust him despite the secrets he kept?

The silence stretched on, heavy and oppressive, until it was broken by the sound of footsteps. Nadeem came bounding over, a plate full of food in his hands and a big grin on his face. "Hey, you two! What's with the long faces? It's a wedding! We should be celebrating!"

He handed them each a piece of cake, hoping to lighten the mood. "I mean, look at this! The bride and groom are having the time of their lives in there, and here we are moping around. Cheer up!"

Ahaan managed a weak smile, accepting the cake. Aliza, still lost in her thoughts, took the cake but didn't eat it. She appreciated Nadeem's attempt to lighten the moment, but the tension between her and Ahaan was palpable.

Nadeem looked between the two of them, sensing that something was off. "Come on, you, guys. Whatever it is, we can figure it out later. Right now, let's just try to enjoy the wedding. We owe it to ourselves to have some fun."

10 - The Aftermath

The marriage concluded in a haze of rituals and ceremonies, but for Aliza, the vibrant celebration had lost its charm. The atmosphere, which had been filled with joy and laughter just a few hours earlier, now felt heavy, almost suffocating. Despite the grandeur of the wedding, with its colorful decorations and the smiling faces of the guests, there was a strange emptiness that clung to the air.

Aliza stood among the crowd, lost in warmth of people but she felt none. Instead, she felt a chill deep inside her, a gnawing unease that had been growing since her conversation with Ahaan outside.

Ahaan had rejoined the wedding after their tense exchange, but he was distant, his usual warmth replaced by a cold detachment. He avoided Aliza's eyes, his expressions shuttered and unreadable. It was as if a wall had suddenly sprung up between them, a barrier she didn't know how to breach. She wanted to reach out to him, to ask him to confide in her, but the look on his face told her that now was not the time.

The rest of the wedding passed in a blur for Aliza. She watched the rituals being performed, heard the cheerful banter around her, but it all seemed far away, as if she were observing it from a distance. Her mind kept replaying the moment when Ahaan had seen Marry, the way his face had drained of color, the panic in his eyes as he bolted from the scene. She had never seen him so rattled, so vulnerable, and it scared her.

What kind of memories was he hiding? Why had Marry's presence triggered such a strong reaction in him? The questions buzzed in her mind like persistent flies, refusing to be swatted away.

Nadeem, usually the life of the party, had also sensed the tension and tried to make light of the situation, cracking jokes and offering his usual witty commentary. But even his efforts couldn't lift the cloud that had settled over them. He could see that Ahaan was struggling with something, something deep and painful, and despite his best efforts to distract them, the underlying tension remained.

Ahaan left the wedding before anyone could say a proper goodbye. He slipped out quietly, avoiding any further interactions. Aliza saw him leave, but by the time she realized what was happening, he was already gone, disappearing into the night like a shadow.

A pang of hurt struck her chest as she watched him go. She had wanted to talk to him, to ask him about Marry, about the memories he had mentioned, but now he was gone, leaving her with nothing but a mess of confused emotions. She pulled out her phone and tried calling him, her heart pounding with each unanswered ring. The call went to voicemail. She tried again, and again, but the result was the same. Ahaan wasn't picking up.

Nadeem noticed her frustration and took out his own phone, dialing Ahaan's number. He walked a few steps away, trying to give her some space, but when he returned, the look on his face told her everything she needed to know. Ahaan wasn't answering his calls either.

"Maybe he just needs some time to himself," Nadeem suggested, though his voice lacked its usual confidence. "He'll come around, Aliza. He always does."

Aliza wanted to believe him, but doubt gnawed at her. She had never seen Ahaan like this before, so withdrawn and secretive. It was as if he had become a stranger overnight, and she didn't know how to reach him.

The rest of the wedding festivities carried on without them, the laughter blending into a background noise that only heightened Aliza's sense of isolation. She felt disconnected from everything around her, her mind too preoccupied with thoughts of Ahaan to engage with the celebrations.

When the last of the guests had departed and the venue began to empty out, Aliza returned to her room, her steps heavy with exhaustion and disappointment. She shut the door behind her and leaned against it, closing her eyes as she tried to make sense of everything that had happened. The evening had started out so beautifully, full of promise and excitement, but it had ended on a note of uncertainty and hurt.

She moved to her bed and sat down, her gaze falling on the notebook she kept on the nightstand. It was her diary, a place where she often poured out her thoughts and feelings, especially on days when the world seemed too overwhelming. Without hesitation, she reached for it, feeling an urgent need to put her emotions into words.

She opened the notebook to a fresh page, the blankness of it a stark contrast to the turmoil inside her. She took a deep breath and began to write.

*****

Dear Diary,

Tonight was supposed to be magical. It was supposed to be a night of joy and celebration, of laughter and dancing, of promises made and futures imagined. But now, as I sit here alone in my room, I can't shake the feeling that something is terribly wrong.

The wedding was beautiful, everything a bride and groom could hope for. The decorations were exquisite, the rituals sacred and moving, the guests all lost in the happiness of the occasion. But for me, all of that faded into the background the moment Ahaan walked out of that door.

I don't know what happened. One moment, we were standing there, watching the rituals and the next, Ahaan was gone, leaving me with nothing but questions and a heart that feels heavier than ever.

What is it that he's hiding? What is it about Marry that scared him so much that he couldn't even stay and face her?

I tried calling him, Nadeem tried calling him, but he won't answer. I can't stop thinking about the look on his face, the way he seemed so lost and afraid. It's like he was drowning in memories, memories that I have no part in, memories that I can't help him with because I don't even know what they are.

And now I'm angry. I'm angry that he won't talk to me, that he just left without a word, leaving me to piece together the puzzle on my own. I thought we were getting closer, that we were building something real and strong, but now I'm not so sure. How can we have a future together when he's keeping secrets from me?

I feel like I'm standing on the edge of something, but I don't know if it's the edge of a cliff or the beginning of a bridge. I want to trust him, I really do, but how can I when he won't even trust me enough to tell me what's going on?

It hurts, diary. It hurts because I care about him so much, and I thought he felt the same. But now I'm not sure where we stand, and it scares me.

I keep replaying the evening in my head, trying to find some clue, some sign that I missed. But all I can remember is the look on his face when he saw Marry, the way he just shut down. What does she mean to him? What kind of memories did she bring back?

I don't want to jump to conclusions, but it's hard not to when he won't tell me anything. I feel like I'm grasping at straws, trying to hold on to something solid in a sea of uncertainty.

Nadeem says he'll come around, that Ahaan just needs time. But what if he doesn't? What if this is the beginning of the end? I hate thinking like that, but I can't help it. I've never felt so unsure, so out of control.

I don't know what to do, diary. I don't know how to fix this, or if it can even be fixed. All I can do is wait and hope that Ahaan will come back to me, that he'll open up and let me in. But the waiting is agony, and the not knowing is even worse.

I'm so angry at him for shutting me out, for leaving me in the dark. But more than that, I'm scared. I'm scared that I might lose him before we even have a chance to really begin.

Please, Ahaan, wherever you are, whatever you're going through, please come back to me. I'm here, and I want to help. But I can't do that if you keep pushing me away.

I just hope he knows that diary. I hope he knows that I'm not going anywhere, that I'll be here when he's ready. But how long can I wait? How long before the uncertainty eats away at what we have?

I guess only time will tell.

*****

Aliza put down her pen, feeling the weight of her words settle over her like a blanket. The anger was still there, simmering beneath the surface, but writing it all down had brought a sense of clarity. She could see now that her anger was rooted in fear, a fear of losing Ahaan, of losing the future she had started to dream about with him.

She closed her diary and placed it back on the nightstand, then lay back on the bed, staring up at the ceiling. The night was quiet now, the distant sounds of the wedding fading into the stillness. But inside her, the storm was far from over.

She reached for her phone one last time, scrolling through her messages. There was nothing from Ahaan, no missed calls, no texts. The emptiness on the screen mirrored the emptiness she felt inside.

Aliza sighed, setting the phone aside. She knew she needed to be patient, to give Ahaan the time he needed to process whatever was going on. But patience was hard when all she wanted was to talk to him, to hear his voice, to know that everything would be okay.

She closed her eyes, willing herself to sleep, but her mind refused to quiet down. Images of the evening flashed before her, each one bringing a fresh wave of doubt and worry.

But amid the chaos of her thoughts, one thing remained clear: she loved Ahaan, and she would wait for him, no matter how long it took. She just hoped that, when he was ready, he would trust her enough to let her in.

As Aliza lay in the darkness, her heart heavy with uncertainty, somewhere out there, Ahaan was grappling with his own demons. The night stretched on, filled with questions and fears, but also with a small, flickering hope that maybe, just maybe, love would be enough to bring them back together.

*****

The sun rose on the horizon, casting a golden hue over the city of Allahabad, but for Aliza, the morning brought little solace. She felt numb, her emotions dulled by the weight of the previous night's events. The vibrant energy of the wedding had dissipated, leaving behind a hollow ache in her chest. She had barely slept, her mind too consumed with thoughts of Ahaan to find any real rest. Now, as she packed her bags to leave Allahabad, a deep sense of unease lingered, wrapping itself around her like a shroud.

She couldn't shake the image of Ahaan's haunted expression, the way he had recoiled at the sight of Marry, the way he had fled the wedding without a word. The unanswered questions gnawed at her, making it impossible to find peace. Aliza knew she needed to give him space, to let him sort through whatever was troubling him, but the distance between them felt like a chasm she couldn't bridge.

As she gathered her belongings, Aliza's mind wandered to Varanasi, the city she had always found comfort in. The idea of returning there was a small comfort, a familiar place where she could collect her thoughts. But the uncertainty about Ahaan continued to weigh heavily on her.

As she zipped up her suitcase, a sudden thought struck her: Manav. The one she thought brought all the books of her from the bookshop. From what little she knew, Manav and Ahaan had been close for years, sharing a bond that went beyond mere friendship. Perhaps Manav knew something about Ahaan's past, something that could shed light on his behavior. Aliza felt a flicker of hope. Maybe Manav could help her understand what was going on.

She made a mental note to reach out to Manav as soon as she was back in Varanasi. But she would need to approach the conversation delicately. She didn't want to betray Ahaan's trust or make him feel like she was prying into his private life. The last thing she wanted was to push him further away.

With a sigh, Aliza grabbed her suitcase and made her way out of the hotel. The streets of Allahabad were already bustling with activity, but she felt disconnected from it all, her thoughts focused on the task ahead. As she settled into the backseat of the car, she stared out the window, watching the city fade into the distance as they drove towards Varanasi.

The journey felt longer than usual, the passing landscape a blur as her mind replayed the events of the previous night. She thought about Ahaan's reaction to Marry, the fear in his eyes, and the way he had shut down completely. What had happened between them? Was it an old flame, a past relationship that had ended badly? Or was it something deeper, something that had scarred him in a way she couldn't understand? Or was it a Love Affair gone wrong? Or was he an unpunished criminal? All these questions were ringing like bells in Aliza's mind constantly. He was a tall, lean man in his early thirties.

The questions swirled in her mind, each one more troubling than the last. She tried to push them aside, to focus on something else, but the knot in her stomach refused to loosen. She couldn't ignore the feeling that something was seriously wrong, that Ahaan was hiding something from her—something that could change everything between them.

By the time she arrived in Varanasi, Aliza felt emotionally drained. The familiar sights of the city, usually so comforting, now felt distant and unreal. She checked into a small guesthouse near the ghats, the same one she had stayed at during her last visit and unpacked her things with a heavy heart. She wondered whether Ahaan was also staying in the same guesthouse or not, but she didn't enquire nor did Nadeem.

Once she was settled, Aliza took a deep breath and reached for her phone. She hesitated for a moment, her fingers hovering over the screen as she debated whether or not to call Manav. What if he didn't know anything? Or worse, what if he did, and it was something she didn't want to hear?

But she knew she couldn't ignore this. She needed answers, and Manav was the only person who might be able to help.

Taking a deep breath, she dialed his number.

The phone rang a few times before Manav answered, his voice cheerful and warm. "Hello?"

"Hi, Manav, it's Aliza," she said, trying to keep her tone light. "I hope I'm not disturbing you."

"Aliza! Not at all. It's great to hear from you," Manav replied. "How are you doing? Are you in Varanasi?"

"Yes, I just got back," Aliza said. "I was actually hoping to catch up with you if you have some time. There's something I'd like to talk about."

"Of course," Manav said, his voice full of curiosity. "I'm free this afternoon. Why don't we meet at the café by the ghat? I'll be there around four."

"That sounds perfect," Aliza agreed, feeling a mixture of relief and apprehension. "I'll see you then."

They exchanged goodbyes, and Aliza hung up the phone, her heart pounding. She had taken the first step, but now she needed to figure out how to approach the conversation without giving too much away. The last thing she wanted was to make things worse for Ahaan or to betray his trust. Nadeem also seemed off. He was not expecting things to turn in such a blizzard manner.

The hours passed slowly as Aliza waited for the meeting with Manav. She tried to distract herself by exploring the ghats and taking in the sights of Varanasi, but her mind kept drifting back to Ahaan and the conversation she was about to have. By the time four o'clock rolled around, she was a bundle of nerves.

Aliza arrived at the café a few minutes early, choosing a table near the window with a view of the river. The sight of the water, calm and steady, helped to ease some of her anxiety. She ordered a cup of Expresso and waited, her thoughts still racing as she rehearsed what she would say.

Manav arrived shortly after, his face lighting up when he saw her.

He was a tall, lean man in his early thirties, with a kind smile and an easygoing demeanor that put Aliza at ease immediately. He greeted her with a warm handshake and sat down across from her, ordering an Americano for himself.

"It's so good to see you again, Aliza," Manav said, taking a sip of his Americano. "I was surprised when you called. Is everything okay?"

Aliza forced a smile, trying to hide the turmoil she felt inside. "It's good to see you too, Manav. Everything's... okay, I guess. I just needed someone to talk to, and I thought of you."

Manav's expression softened with concern. "You can talk to me about anything, Aliza. What's on your mind?"

Aliza hesitated, unsure of how to begin. She didn't want to dive straight into the issue with Ahaan, but she also didn't want to beat around the bush. Taking a deep breath, she decided to start with something more general.

"I've been thinking a lot about Ahaan lately," she began, her voice steady. "He's a wonderful person, and we've grown really close. But lately, I've noticed that he's been... distant. Something's bothering him, and I can't figure out what it is."

Manav nodded, listening intently. "Ahaan can be a bit of a mystery sometimes," he said thoughtfully. "He's always been one to keep his feelings to himself, especially when it comes to things that are painful for him."

Aliza looked down at her cup, her fingers tracing the rim. "Do you know if there's anything from his past that might be causing him distress and confinement? Something that he hasn't dealt with?"

Manav's expression grew more serious, and he leaned back in his chair, considering her question. "Ahaan's been through a lot," he said after a moment. "He doesn't talk about it much, but there are things in his past that have left deep scars. I've always respected his privacy, so I haven't pried, but I've seen how those memories affect him."

Aliza felt a pang of sympathy for Ahaan, but also a sense of frustration. "I just wish he would open up to me," she said softly. "I want to help him, to be there for him, but I don't know how to do that when he won't let me in."

Manav reached out and gave a reassuring nod. "I understand, Aliza. It's hard when someone you care about is hurting, and you feel helpless. But Ahaan's always been someone who deals with things on his own terms. It's not that he doesn't trust you—it's just that he doesn't know how to share his pain."

Aliza looked up at Manav, her eyes searching his. "Do you know anything about his relationship with someone named Marry?" she asked cautiously, not wanting to reveal too much but hoping for some insight.

Manav's brows furrowed in confusion. "Marry? No… haven't heard about this name before? Why are you asking?"

Aliza's heart sank a little, disappointment mingling with her concern. "I thought maybe you'd know something. He seemed really shaken when he saw her at the wedding, but I have no idea why. It's like something inside him just broke, and I don't know how to help him."

Manav leaned back in his chair, a thoughtful look crossing his face. "Ahaan's always been a private person," he said slowly. "He doesn't share much about his past, even with those he's close to. But if seeing this Marry affected him so deeply, there's got to be something significant there, something that he's kept buried for a long time."

Aliza bit her lip, feeling more lost than ever. "I wish I knew how to get through to him, how to make him open up. He's been so distant since that night, and I'm afraid he's pulling away from me."

Manav nodded understandingly. "It's hard when someone you care about is hurting, and you don't know how to help. But sometimes, the best thing you can do is just be there for him, even if he's not ready to talk yet. Let him know that you're there, ready to listen when he's ready to share."

Aliza sighed, her heart heavy with worry. "I care about him so much, Manav. I don't want him to feel like he has to go through this alone."

Manav reached out offering a reassuring smile. "You're doing the right thing by being there for him, Aliza. Ahaan needs to know that he's not alone, even if he's not ready to face whatever's haunting him."

Aliza returned his smile, though it was tinged with uncertainty. "But how do I reach him? How do I help him if he won't let me in?"

Manav paused, then seemed to come to a decision. "There might be someone who can help you understand Ahaan better," he said carefully. "Ahaan has a sister—well, a long-distance sister, actually—who lives in Delhi. They're very close to each other, but I've only met her a couple of times. She might know more about his past than I do."

Aliza was intrigued and asked "A sister? I didn't even know he had one."

Manav nodded. "They don't talk much now, and she's not someone Ahaan brings up often, but if you're looking for answers, she might be able to help. Her name is Rhea. I can give you her number if you want."

Aliza felt a flicker of hope. This could be the key to understanding what Ahaan was going through. "That would be really helpful, Manav. I'd appreciate it."

Manav pulled out his phone, quickly scrolling through his contacts before finding Rhea's number. He wrote it down on a piece of paper and handed it to Aliza. "Just be gentle with her. Like I said, they're not very close, and I'm not sure how much she'll be willing to share. But it's worth a try."

Aliza took the paper, carefully tucking it into her bag. "Thank you, Manav. I'm not sure what I'll say to her, but I know I have to try."

"You're welcome, Aliza," Manav said with a warm smile. "I hope you find the answers you're looking for. Just remember, whatever happens, Ahaan is lucky to have someone like you who cares so much."

They finished their drinks and chatted for a while longer, the conversation shifting to lighter topics as the tension began to ease. By the time they parted ways, Aliza felt a little more at peace. She still didn't have all the answers, but at least she had a new direction to pursue.

As she walked back to the guesthouse, Aliza couldn't help but feel a renewed sense of determination. She loved Ahaan, and she wasn't going to give up on him. Whatever demons he was facing, she would be there for him, ready to support him whenever he was ready to open up.

For now, all she could do was wait and hope that reaching out to Rhea might provide the key to unlocking the mysteries of Ahaan's past—and that their love would be strong enough to withstand whatever came next.

11 - Knowing The Unknown

Aliza sat on the edge of her bed; her phone cradled in her hands as she stared at Rhea's number. The paper Manav had given her was now crumpled from her repeated folding and unfolding, a clear indication of the turmoil inside her. The conversation with Manav had opened a door, but it was a door she was hesitant to walk through. What if Rhea didn't want to talk? What if Ahaan had the scars of an untold broken relationship/affair? What if Ahaan found out she had contacted his stepsister behind his back? The fear of potentially hurting Ahaan weighed heavily on her heart, but so did the need to understand what had driven him away from her at the wedding.

After what felt like hours of internal debate, Aliza took a deep breath and dialed the number. Her heart pounded with every ring. Each second that passed only heightened her anxiety, and just as she was about to hang up, a soft voice answered on the other end.

Aliza's fingers trembled as she dialed the number, the weight of her uncertainty pressing down on her like a heavy blanket. She had been debating this call for days, going back and forth in her mind, trying to figure out if it was even the right thing to do. But with each passing day, her concern for Ahaan had grown stronger, more urgent, until she could no longer ignore it. She needed answers, and if there was anyone who could provide them, it was Rhea.

The phone rang twice, and then a voice answered. "Hello?"

Aliza's breath caught in her throat, her heart pounding so loudly she could barely hear herself think. She had rehearsed this moment in her mind, but now that it was here, the words seemed to escape her. "Hi, is this Rhea?" she managed to ask, her voice trembling slightly.

"Yes, this is Rhea. Who's this?" Rhea's tone was polite but cautious, as if she were bracing herself for whatever was about to come.

Aliza swallowed hard, trying to steady her nerves. "This is Aliza. I'm… I'm a friend of Ahaan's. Manav gave me your number." She winced slightly at how shaky her voice sounded, wishing she could project more confidence, but the truth was she felt anything but confident right now.

There was a brief pause on the other end of the line, just long enough for Aliza to wonder if Rhea was about to hang up. "Ahaan's friend? How can I help you?" Rhea's tone remained polite, but there was an edge to it now, a guardedness that made Aliza even more aware of the delicate nature of the conversation she was about to have.

Aliza hesitated, her mind racing. How could she possibly explain what she was feeling without sounding like a complete stranger meddling in someone else's life? But then she remembered the look in Ahaan's eyes at the wedding, the way he had suddenly withdrawn, as if retreating into himself, and she knew she couldn't back out now.

"I'm sorry to bother you, Rhea," Aliza began, her voice soft but sincere. "I know we've never met, and this might seem strange, but I'm really worried about Ahaan." She paused, trying to find the right words. "There's something I need to know about him, and Manav told me that only you could help me, and that's why I'm calling you."

There was a long silence, and Aliza could feel her heart pounding faster with each passing second. She knew she was asking a lot of Rhea, a complete stranger, but she also knew that she had no other choice. She needed to understand what was going on with Ahaan, and if that meant stepping into uncomfortable territory, then so be it.

Rhea finally spoke, her voice firm but not unkind. "Just say it. Don't beat around the bush. If Manav says I can help, then I'll do my best."

Aliza took a deep breath, feeling the weight of what she was about to say pressing down on her. She had to choose her words carefully, but at the same time, she knew she couldn't hold anything back. "We were at a wedding recently, Ahaan and me," she began, her words rushing out in a single breath. "And he saw someone there—a woman named Marry. After that, he became really distant, and then he just left. I tried calling him, but he won't answer. I don't know what's going on, and I thought maybe you could help me understand."

The words hung in the air between them, heavy with unspoken fears and unanswered questions. Aliza could hear her own breath in the silence that followed, could feel her heart racing as she waited for Rhea's response. She had no idea how Rhea would react, whether she would be offended or defensive, or whether she would even have the answers Aliza was so desperately seeking.

There was another silence on the other end of the line. Aliza could almost hear Rhea weighing her words, deciding how much to share with this stranger who had suddenly appeared in her life.

"I'm sorry, Aliza," Rhea finally said. "But I don't know anything about a Marry. Ahaan never mentioned her to me, and I can't say I've ever heard that name before. But…" She hesitated, as if unsure whether to continue. "But if you're asking me about Ahaan, there's something you should know. It might not be related, but it's something that's always haunted him."

Aliza's heart skipped a beat. She leaned forward, her grip tightening on the phone. "Please, Rhea. Anything you can tell me might help. I just want to understand."

Rhea sighed, and Aliza could sense the sadness in her voice. "Ahaan and I… we were close when we were younger. But things changed a few years ago. We don't talk much anymore, and I always wondered why. It wasn't until recently that I started to piece things together. You see, Ahaan has a phobia—a fear that I didn't realize the extent of until it became too late to fix."

"A phobia?" Aliza echoed, puzzled. "What kind of phobia?"

There was a brief pause before Rhea spoke again, her voice softer this time. "He's terrified of pregnant women. It's something that makes him uncontrollably anxious, even strange. I didn't understand it myself until I experienced it firsthand. When I got pregnant with my first child, Ahaan… he just disappeared from my life. He stopped calling, stopped visiting. It was like I didn't exist to him anymore."

Aliza's mind whirled, trying to process what she was hearing. "But why? Why would he be afraid of pregnant women?"

"I don't know," Rhea admitted, her voice tinged with regret. "He never told me. Whenever I tried to talk to him about it, he would shut down or change the subject. It hurts, Aliza. It hurts to lose my brother, especially at a time when I needed him the most. But I couldn't force him to confront whatever it was that made him act that way. And eventually, I just… gave up."

Aliza felt a knot form in her stomach. Ahaan, the man she had fallen in love with, had been carrying this burden for so long, and she had never known. But what could have happened to cause such a deep-seated fear? She tried to imagine the kind of trauma or experience that could lead to such a phobia, but her mind drew a blank.

"Rhea, I'm so sorry you had to go through that," Aliza said softly.

"It must have been so difficult for you."

"It was," Rhea replied, her voice steady but sad. "But I've learned to live with it. I just wish things had been different between us. I miss my brother, Aliza. I miss the way things used to be."

Aliza's heart ached for Rhea. She could hear the longing in her voice, the pain of a relationship lost to something neither of them understood. "Do you think… do you think there's any way to help him? To make him confront whatever it is that's causing this?"

"I don't know," Rhea said after a moment of silence. "It would have to be something he wants to face, something he's ready to deal with. I've tried talking to him in the past, but he always brushed me off. Maybe he'll open up to you, though. You're not family, so he might feel more comfortable talking to you."

Aliza nodded, even though Rhea couldn't see her. "I hope so. I just don't want to push him away by bringing it up too soon. But I can't just ignore it, either. It's affecting him, and it's affecting our relationship."

"You're in a tough spot, Aliza," Rhea acknowledged, her tone sympathetic. "But if you love Ahaan, and I believe you do, then you'll find a way to support him without pushing him too hard. Just be patient and let him know that you're there for him when he's ready to talk."

Aliza felt a wave of gratitude wash over her. Despite the distance between them, Rhea was offering her advice and support, even though she had every reason to resent the situation. "Thank you, Rhea. I can't tell you how much I appreciate this. I didn't know what to expect when I called you, but you've given me a lot to think about."

"You're welcome," Rhea said with a small, sad smile in her voice. "I hope you can help Ahaan, Aliza. I hope you can help him find the peace he needs."

They exchanged a few more words before saying their goodbyes, and Aliza hung up the phone, her mind racing. She stared at the screen, the weight of Rhea's revelation settling heavily on her shoulders. Ahaan had a phobia—an irrational, intense fear—that had driven a wedge between him and his stepsister. And now it was threatening to do the same between him and Aliza.

As she sat there, lost in thought, Aliza couldn't help but replay the events of the past few days in her mind. Ahaan's sudden departure from the wedding, his refusal to answer her calls, the fear in his eyes when he saw Marry… it all made sense now. But it also raised more questions than it answered. What had happened to Ahaan that made him so afraid of pregnant women? And why hadn't he ever mentioned it to her? She remembered the other time when she met Ahaan in a cafe and a lady was sitting on the next table, she was also pregnant and there was a strange fear in Ahaan's eyes. Now everything made sense but still nothing made any sense. Why is the question that lingered.

Aliza felt a pang of guilt. She had been so focused on her own confusion and hurt that she hadn't considered what Ahaan might be going through. But now that she knew, she was determined to find a way to help him, even if it meant facing the darkness of his past.

The next few days passed in a blur. Aliza tried to reach out to Ahaan, but her calls went unanswered, and her messages were left unread. She wanted to give him space, but the uncertainty gnawed at her, making it difficult to focus on anything else. She thought about going to see him in person, but she didn't want to risk pushing him further away.

Instead, Aliza found herself returning to her notebook, the pages filled with her thoughts and fears. Writing had always been a way for her to process her emotions, and now, more than ever, she needed an outlet for the confusion and worry that consumed her.

She wrote about the wedding, about the way Ahaan's hand had trembled when he saw Marry, about the look in his eyes as he fled the scene. She wrote about her conversation with Rhea, the pain in the woman's voice as she spoke about losing her brother to an inexplicable fear. And she wrote about her own feelings—the love she had for Ahaan, the fear of losing him to something she couldn't understand, and the determination to stand by him no matter what.

Days turned into weeks, and still, there was no word from Ahaan. Aliza tried to be patient, tried to respect his need for space, but the silence was suffocating. She felt like she was walking on a tightrope, balancing her love for Ahaan with the fear that she might never get through to him.

Finally, after what felt like an eternity, Aliza received a text from Ahaan. It was short, just a few words, but it was enough to send her heart racing.

"Can we talk? I'm ready now."

Aliza's fingers trembled as she typed her response. **"Of course. Whenever you're ready."**

12 - Ahaan's Past

A few days earlier, after the wedding: Ahaan sat alone in his room, his body tense with a mix of emotions he could barely name. The soft glow of the evening light filtered through the curtains, casting long shadows across the floor, but they did nothing to dispel the darkness that seemed to seep into his very soul. The silence around him was deafening, an oppressive weight that pressed down on him from all sides. It was as if the air itself was thick with unspoken words, with feelings he had long buried but could never truly forget.

Since the wedding, he had kept to himself, retreating into the familiar confines of his solitude. He had avoided everyone— Manav, his family, and most of all, Aliza. He knew she was worried, that she was confused by his sudden withdrawal. He could see the questions in her eyes, the unspoken pleas for him to let her in, to share whatever it was that was tearing him apart inside. But he couldn't. How could he possibly explain to her the storm that raged within him, the memories that haunted him, the irrational fear that had controlled him for as long as he could remember?

The phobia had its roots deep in his childhood, in a time when the world was a much simpler place, yet far more terrifying. He had been only four years old when his mother became pregnant with his younger sibling. At first, the news had filled him with a childlike wonder. He had been excited, thrilled by the idea of having a little brother or sister to play with. He had imagined all the games they would play, the secrets they would share, the adventures they would embark on together. In his young mind, it was a magical time, a time of possibility and joy.

But as the months went by, that excitement began to fade, replaced by a growing sense of confusion. His mother, the woman who had always been his safe haven, his source of love and comfort, began to change. She was no longer the patient, gentle figure he had always known. Instead, she became irritable, her moods swinging wildly from one extreme to the other. She would scold him for things that had never bothered her before— spilled milk, toys left on the floor, the way he spoke too loudly or too softly. Every little mistake seemed to provoke her anger, and Ahaan, too young to understand what was happening, was left bewildered and hurt.

He didn't know why his mother had changed, why the person he loved most in the world was suddenly so distant, so angry. He could only see that her growing belly seemed to coincide with her growing irritation, and in his young mind, the two became inextricably linked. The baby, the sibling he had once been so excited about, now represented something dark and frightening. It represented a loss of his mother's love, of her patience, of the warmth that had once filled their home.

Ahaan's confusion gradually turned to fear. He began to dread the moments when his mother's irritation would flare up, when her voice would take on that sharp, cutting edge that made him feel small and powerless. He tried to be good, to be quiet, to stay out of her way, but nothing seemed to help. The more he tried to please her, the more he seemed to provoke her anger. And the more he provoked her anger, the more he came to associate her growing belly with a sense of dread.

It wasn't long before that dread began to take on a life of its own. It seeped into his dreams, turning them into nightmares from which he would wake up trembling and afraid. He would lie in bed, staring at the shadows on the ceiling, his heart racing as he imagined the baby inside his mother's belly growing larger and larger, pushing her further and further away from him. He felt as if he was losing her, bit by bit, and there was nothing he could do to stop it.

As he grew older, those memories became more distant, blurred at the edges by time. But the fear remained, buried deep within him, a constant undercurrent in his life. He didn't understand it, didn't know why the sight of a pregnant woman could send his heart racing, why it made his palms sweat and his breath come in short, panicked gasps. All he knew was that it was something he couldn't control, something that made him feel weak and ashamed.

He had never told anyone about his phobia. How could he? It was so irrational, so inexplicable, that he could barely explain it to himself, let alone to someone else. He had learned to hide it, to bury it deep inside where no one could see it. But it was always there, lurking in the shadows of his mind, ready to spring to life at the slightest provocation.

And now, with Aliza, it was worse than ever. He cared about her—more than he had ever cared about anyone before. She was kind, patient, and understanding in a way that made him feel safe, made him feel like he could finally let down his guard. But that only made his fear more potent, more paralyzing. How could he let her see this dark, twisted part of himself? How could he expect her to understand something that he couldn't even understand himself?

Ahaan's thoughts were a tangled mess, a storm of emotions that he couldn't untangle. He wanted to talk to her, to explain what was going on inside his head, but every time he tried, the words caught in his throat. He was trapped by his own fear, by the memories of a time he had tried so hard to forget.

He leaned back against the pillows, his eyes closing as he let out a long, shaky breath. He couldn't keep doing this—couldn't keep pushing her away, couldn't keep hiding from his own feelings. But the thought of opening up to her, of letting her see the broken parts of himself, terrified him more than anything.

In the quiet of his room, Ahaan's mind drifted back to those early days, to the little boy he had once been. He could still see himself, small and scared, standing at the edge of his mother's bed, watching as she rubbed her swollen belly with a distant, distracted look in her eyes. He could still hear the sharpness in her voice as she scolded him for something trivial, something that didn't matter. And he could still feel the sting of her words, the way they had cut deep into his heart, leaving scars that had never fully healed.

*****

When he saw Marry at the wedding, pregnant and glowing with happiness, that old fear came rushing back with a force that left him shaken. He had to get away, had to escape before the memories overwhelmed him. But now, sitting alone in his room, he knew that running away wouldn't solve anything. He needed to face this, to understand where this fear came from and why it still had such a hold on him.

But how could he explain all of this to Aliza? How could he make her understand something that he himself didn't fully grasp? He loved her, more than he had ever loved anyone, and the thought of losing her because of this irrational fear terrified him. But he couldn't keep running forever. He couldn't keep this part of himself hidden from her if they were going to have a future together.

Ahaan reached for his notebook, the one place where he could pour out his feelings without fear of judgment. He had always found solace in writing, in turning his emotions into words that somehow made them more manageable. Tonight, he needed that solace more than ever. He began to write, the words flowing from him as if they had been waiting for this moment to be released.

In the quiet of the night, I think of you,
Of all the things I wish I could convey.
Yet shadows dance, obscuring true,
And silence echoes, a mournful fray.

I want to tell you all I feel,
To bare my soul, without a mask.
But fear, a heavy, chilling steel,
Holds me in chains, a heavy task.

You are the light in my life,
the warmth in my cold,
Yet I am lost in a storm,
unable to find my way.

You are the light,
the warmth I crave,
Yet lost I wander, cold and dark.
I see your love, a beacon brave,
But shadows hide, a haunting mark.
This fear, a ghost from days of yore,
A part of me I cannot mend,
Scares me to depths, to very core,
If you look closely, to the end.

But love for you, it burns so bright,
Beyond all words, it sets me free.
I pray one day, with all my might,
To find the strength, to confess to thee.

For now, I hope you'll stay with me,
See through the fear, the pain I bear.
Without you, lost and wild I'll be,
A soul adrift, beyond repair.

Ahaan put down his pen, his heart heavy with the weight of his unspoken words. Writing the poem had brought him some relief, but it hadn't lessened the fear gnawing at his insides. He knew he couldn't keep this up forever. Eventually, he would have to talk to Aliza, to tell her everything, but he wasn't ready yet. Not tonight.

He thought back to his mother, to the woman she had been before that fateful pregnancy. She had always been kind, nurturing, the center of his world. But when she became pregnant, something changed. Ahaan had tried so hard to be good, to do everything right, but nothing he did seemed to please her. The more she scolded him, the more he retreated into himself, unable to understand why his mother, who had once been his greatest source of comfort, had become a source of fear.

He had never told anyone about those feelings. Not his friends, not Aliza, not even himself, really. He had pushed those memories so deep that they had become almost forgotten, until now. Now, they were all he could think about, and the pain was as fresh as it had been all those years ago.

Ahaan closed his eyes and took a deep breath, trying to calm the storm inside him. He thought of his mother, of the woman she had become after his sibling was born—loving, patient, the mother he had always known. But the damage had already been done. The fear had already taken root in his heart, and no matter how much she loved him, it couldn't erase the trauma of those nine months.

He picked up his pen again, feeling the need to write, to try to make sense of the tangled emotions that were tearing him apart. This time, the words were for his mother.

Mother, do you recall those days of old,
When in your arms, I'd seek your gentle hold?
Your voice, a melody that soothed my fears,
A lullaby that chased away my tears.
I was your child, so innocent, so small,
In your embrace, I felt I had it all.
But then the skies turned grey, the light grew dim,
And love that once was bright, began to thin.
You carried life, a blessing deep inside,
But with it came a storm you couldn't hide.

The warmth between us chilled, began to fade,
And in your eyes, I saw a love betrayed.
I tried to be the son you'd always known,
But every smile I gave, you met with stone.
I didn't understand the shift in you,
Why laughter ceased, and distance only grew.
Now, though I'm grown, those shadows still remain,
A phantom in my heart, a ghost of pain.
I long to tell you, Mother, all my grief,
But words fall short, and silence brings relief.
I know you loved, and in your way, you cared,
But in those moments, love felt unrepaired.
I seek to forgive, to mend the broken thread,
But memories of old still linger in my head.
Mother, I yearn for days of light and grace,
When love was clear, and joy adorned your face.
Yet here I stand, a prisoner of the past,
Wishing for peace, for shadows not to last.
So here I plead, with heart both torn and true,
To find a way to heal, and start anew.
For though the wounds run deep, and scars remain,
I wish to rise above the silent pain.

Ahaan set down the pen, his hand trembling. The words had come from a place deep within him, a place he rarely allowed himself to visit. Writing them had brought some clarity, but it had also reopened old wounds that he had never fully healed.

He sat in the silence, the weight of his past pressing down on him. He knew he couldn't keep this to himself forever. He would have to tell Aliza, to let her in on the secret that had haunted him for so long. But the thought of doing so terrified him. What if she didn't understand? What if she couldn't accept this part of him?

The fear of losing her was almost as strong as the fear itself. Ahaan knew he was at a crossroads. He could continue to hide, to keep this part of himself locked away, but that would mean losing Aliza. Or he could face his fears, confront the past, and hope that she would still love him despite everything.

Days passed, and Ahaan continued to wrestle with his thoughts. He avoided Aliza, not because he didn't want to see her, but because he was afraid of what might happen if he did. He knew she was worried, that she deserved an explanation, but he couldn't bring himself to face her.

Finally, after weeks of agonizing over what to do, Ahaan made a decision. He couldn't keep running from his past, and he couldn't keep pushing Aliza away. If there was any hope for their future together, he needed to be honest with her. He needed to tell her everything, even if it meant risking her rejection.

He picked up his phone and hesitated for a moment, his heart pounding in his chest. Then, with a deep breath, he messaged on Aliza's number:

"Can we talk? I'm ready now."

Aliza's fingers trembled as she typed her response. **"Of course. Whenever you're ready."**

13 - Sorting Things Out

They agreed to meet at a quiet café on the outskirts of the city, a place that held memories of simpler times, when their relationship was still new and filled with unspoken promises. The café was nestled between old, towering trees, their leaves rustling softly in the breeze. It was an old brick building, with ivy climbing up the walls and a wooden sign hanging above the entrance that read "Whispering Pines." The name suited the place well—it was a refuge, a sanctuary where the outside world seemed to fade away, leaving only the sound of whispered conversations and the clinking of coffee cups.

Aliza walked down the path that led to the café's entrance, her heart pounding in her chest. The familiar scent of freshly brewed coffee and baked goods greeted her as she pushed open the heavy wooden door. Inside, the café was dimly lit, with warm, golden lights hanging from the ceiling, casting a soft glow over the rustic wooden furniture. The walls were adorned with old photographs and paintings, each one telling a story of its own.

Her eyes scanned the room, and she spotted Ahaan sitting at a corner table, his gaze fixed on the window. He was always drawn to that spot, where he could watch the world outside while still feeling cocooned in the café's warmth. Today, though, he looked different. The man she saw now was a shadow of the one she had known. His shoulders were slumped, as if carrying the weight of the world, and his eyes, once so full of life, were clouded with a weariness that hadn't been there before.

Ahaan's fingers tapped rhythmically on the table, a subtle sign of his nervousness. He had chosen a simple black shirt, the sleeves rolled up to his elbows, revealing the faint lines of veins that pulsed beneath his skin. His hair, usually tousled in that charming, careless way, looked like it hadn't been touched in days, lying flat against his forehead. The sunlight streaming through the window cast long shadows across his face, highlighting the tiredness etched into his features. But when he looked up and saw her standing at the entrance, there was something else in his eyes—something that looked like resolve, a determination to face what he had been running from.

"Aliza," Ahaan said softly as she approached the table. His voice was low, almost hesitant, as if he were unsure of how to begin.

She smiled, though it was tinged with concern, and slid into the seat opposite him. "Ahaan," she replied, her voice equally soft. She reached across the table, her fingers brushing against his, a small gesture of reassurance.

For a moment, neither of them spoke. The café around them hummed with quiet activity—the soft murmur of other patrons, the clatter of dishes in the kitchen, the hiss of the espresso machine. But at their table, there was only silence, heavy with the things left unsaid.

Ahaan finally broke the silence, his gaze dropping to where their hands touched. "I'm sorry, Aliza. For everything." His voice was thick with emotion, and she could see the struggle in his eyes, the battle between wanting to pull away and wanting to finally let her in.

She squeezed his hand gently. "I know you've been going through something, Ahaan. I just wish you would talk to me. I'm here for you, no matter what it is."

Ahaan took a deep breath, as if gathering the courage to speak. "It's not easy to explain. I've been dealing with something— something I've never told anyone about. It's... it's been with me for as long as I can remember, and I don't even fully understand it myself."

Aliza's heart ached at the vulnerability in his voice. She had always known there was something deeper, something that haunted him, but hearing him admit it was both heartbreaking and a relief. "You don't have to go through it alone, Ahaan. Whatever it is, we can face it together."

He looked up at her, his eyes glistening with unshed tears. "It's not that simple, Aliza. It's something from my past, something I've buried for so long that I thought I could just forget about it. But I can't. It's always there, in the back of my mind, and it's been affecting everything—my relationships, my life, even how I feel about myself."

She listened intently, her heart breaking a little more with each word he spoke. "What happened, Ahaan?" she asked gently, giving him the space to continue at his own pace.

Ahaan let out a shaky breath, his fingers gripping the edge of the table as if it were the only thing keeping him grounded. "It started when I was a child. My mother... she was pregnant with my younger sibling when I was about four years old. At first, I was excited, you know? The idea of having a little brother or sister was... magical. But then things changed."

He paused; his gaze distant as he was drawn back into the memories that had haunted him for so long. "My mother, she wasn't the same during that pregnancy. She became... irritable, angry, like everything I did was wrong. She would scold me for the smallest things, things that never mattered before. And as a four-year-old, I couldn't understand why. All I knew was that the person who had always been my safe place was suddenly pushing me away."

Aliza's heart clenched as she imagined a young Ahaan, confused and hurt, unable to comprehend why his mother was treating him so harshly. She wanted to reach out to that little boy, to comfort him, to tell him it wasn't his fault.

Ahaan continued, his voice growing softer. "I started to associate her growing belly with her anger. In my mind, the baby was the reason she didn't love me anymore. And over time, that fear, that association, it grew into something darker. I didn't realize it then, but it planted the seeds of a phobia—a fear of pregnant women."

He looked up at her, his eyes filled with shame. "I know it sounds irrational. I know it doesn't make sense. But every time I see a pregnant woman, I'm reminded of that time, of how my mother's love seemed to slip away from me. It's like I'm that little boy again, scared and alone, thinking I've done something wrong."

Aliza felt tears prickling at the corners of her eyes, but she forced herself to stay composed, to be strong for him. "Ahaan," she whispered, "you were just a child. You couldn't have known what was really happening. Your mother's behavior wasn't your fault."

He nodded, though he seemed unconvinced. "I know that logically. But the fear is still there. It's like it's etched into my very being. And it's been affecting everything—how I relate to others, how I handle relationships. It's why I pulled away from you after the wedding. Seeing that woman, Marry, it brought all of those old feelings back to the surface, and I didn't know how to deal with them."

Aliza reached out, taking both of his hands in hers. "You don't have to deal with it alone, Ahaan. I'm here. We can work through this together, step by step. You're not that little boy anymore, and you don't have to be afraid of losing love."

He squeezed her hands tightly, as if drawing strength from her words. "I've kept this hidden for so long, Aliza. I've never told anyone about it, not even my family. I was too ashamed, too afraid of what people would think. But with you... I want to try. I want to try and face this, to let go of the fear."

She smiled, a tear slipping down her cheek. "We'll face it together, Ahaan. You're not alone in this."

For a moment, they sat in silence, their hands clasped together across the table, the connection between them stronger than ever. The world outside the window continued on as usual—people walked by, cars drove past—but inside the café, time seemed to stand still.

Ahaan felt a weight lift off his shoulders, a sense of relief that came from finally sharing the burden he had carried for so long. He knew the journey ahead wouldn't be easy, that there would be challenges and setbacks, but for the first time in years, he felt like he wasn't facing it alone. He had Aliza by his side, and that gave him hope.

Taking a deep breath, he began to speak again, his voice steadier now. "There's something I want to share with you. It's a poem I wrote... for my mother. I've never shown it to anyone before, but I think... maybe it's time. It's immature but nothing feels like truer than this to me. I was only 5 years old when I wrote this and has kept with me till now. You are the first person I am sharing this with."

Aliza took the poem and read it:

Mommy, why are you mad at me?
I didn't mean to spill my juice, you see.
Your face is different, not like before,
You don't smile at me anymore.
Your tummy is growing big and round,
But why do you frown when I'm around?
I just want to play and be your friend,
But now I'm scared, will this ever end?
I miss your hugs, warm and tight,
When you'd tuck me in and say goodnight.
Now you're always tired and sad,
Did I do something to make you mad?
I'm sorry if I made you cry,
I just don't understand why.

I'll be good, I promise, I swear,
I just want to know that you still care.
Please don't be angry, please don't be mean,
I want things to be like they've always been.
I love you, Mommy, more than you know,
I just wish the old you would show.

As Aliza finished reading the poem, she sat back, her eyes wide and unblinking. The words on the page were a glimpse into Ahaan's childhood, revealing a vulnerability and fear that was both poignant and unsettling. It was difficult to reconcile the vibrant, assured Ahaan she knew with the frightened child whose world had been overshadowed by his mother's anger and her growing belly. The poem, with its raw simplicity and childlike innocence, painted a vivid picture of a young boy's anguish—an anguish that had silently shaped Ahaan's life.

Aliza's gaze shifted from the paper to Ahaan, who was watching her intently, his face a mix of hope and trepidation. She could feel the weight of his unspoken pain, the kind of pain that could only be masked by a brave face and a cheerful demeanor. The realization hit her hard; the man she loved had been living with a ghostly memory, one that had shadowed his every interaction with pregnant women and, by extension, with life itself.

Trying to keep her voice steady, Aliza asked, "Ahaan, didn't you ever talk to your father about this? I mean, he must have noticed something was wrong. Why didn't you reach out for help?"

Aahan's shoulders sagged slightly as he looked away, the shadows of past hurt flickering across his face. "My father was dedicated to his country," he said quietly, his voice tinged with a hint of sadness. "Being an army man, he was often away on duty. When he was home, he was usually exhausted, and maybe... maybe that made things worse for my mother. His absence meant she had to handle everything on her own, and I think it only added to her frustration."

He paused, taking a deep breath before continuing. "When my father was around, his focus was always on his work. He was a good man, dedicated and honorable, but he wasn't always there to see the struggle at home. I didn't want to add to his burden, especially when he was already so strained from his duties. And my mother... well, she was dealing with her own challenges. I thought I should just manage on my own, keep my fears to myself."

Aliza's heart ached at the depth of Ahaan's isolation. She reached across the table, gently placing her hand over his. "Ahaan, you don't have to manage alone anymore. I'm here for you, and we can face this together. You don't need to keep these feelings buried."

Aahan looked up at her, his eyes reflecting a mixture of gratitude and sorrow. "Thank you, Aliza. I've been so afraid of discussing, of being judged or misunderstood. But knowing that you're here for me, that you care... it means more than I can put into words."

Aliza's expression softened as she squeezed his hand. "You don't have to explain everything all at once. Just know that I'm with you, and I want to help you heal from this. We'll take it one step at a time."

A faint, grateful smile touched Ahaan's lips. For the first time in a long while, he felt a glimmer of hope. With Aliza's support, he might finally find the strength to confront the past and move forward. The journey ahead would be challenging, but with Aliza by his side, he felt that he could begin to unravel the layers of pain that had been hidden for so long.

As they sat together in the quiet café, the weight of Ahaan's fears seemed a little lighter, and the path to healing seemed just a bit clearer.

Ahaan's gaze wandered absently as he broke the silence. "By the way, Aliza, have you seen Nadeem lately?"

Aliza tilted her head slightly, her brow furrowing in thought. "Actually, no. I haven't seen him for a while either. He's been so engrossed in his phone calls and spending a lot of time at the cybercafé. He's always busy with something, probably playing video games or chatting with friends."

Ahaan's lips curved into a small, knowing smile. "Ah, that's Nadeem for you. Always up to something."

Aliza raised an eyebrow, curiosity raised. "Why do you ask? Is everything okay?"

Ahaan's expression grew thoughtful. "I was just wondering if you could do me a favor. When you see Nadeem next, could you ask him to return something to me? It's my diary of poems."

Aliza blinked, surprised by the request. "Your diary? Why would Nadeem have it?"

Ahaan's expression grew thoughtful, a shadow of unease passing over his face. "After the wedding, things got a bit hectic. Nadeem came to see me, wanting to talk. I was overwhelmed, not really in the mood to engage. I guess I just needed some time to myself. I remember Nadeem's eyes landing on my diary of poems, the one I keep close to my heart."

Aliza's curiosity deepened. "So, what happened?"

Ahaan sighed, rubbing his temples as if trying to erase the memory. "Nadeem seemed unusually intense that day, more so than usual. He was looking around the room, and then he saw the diary lying on my desk. I noticed him eyeing it for a moment, but I was too caught up in my own thoughts to stop him."

Aliza's eyes widened. "He took the diary?"

"Yes," Ahaan confirmed, his voice tinged with frustration. "I saw him pick it up and slip it into his bag. He probably thought I didn't notice, but I did. I was too exhausted to confront him or ask him why he was taking it. I just let him go, hoping it was a temporary thing."

Aliza's confusion grew. "That's strange. Nadeem's not usually like this. He's never shown an interest in your poetry before."

Ahaan nodded; his expression pained. "I know. That's what made it even more unsettling. I don't understand why he would take it without asking. It was like something shifted in him after the wedding. I can't shake the feeling that there's more to it than just curiosity."

Aliza's mind raced, trying to piece together the puzzle. "Nadeem has been acting oddly lately—always busy with his phone, spending hours at the cybercafé. It's not like him to be so secretive. Maybe he's going through something himself."

Ahaan's gaze softened, and he nodded slowly. "It's possible. I've been so wrapped up in my own struggles that I didn't consider what might be going on with him. But if you do see him, please ask him to return my diary. It's important to me, not just for the poems, but for what it represents—my past, my fears, my memories."

Aliza reached out, placing a comforting hand on Ahaan's. "I'll talk to him, Ahaan. I promise. We'll get to the bottom of this."

Ahaan gave her a grateful smile, his eyes reflecting a mix of relief and apprehension. "Thank you, Aliza. I appreciate it more than you know."

Before leaving the café Aliza approached quietly, her footsteps light against the gravel path. She had seen that look in his eyes before, a sadness he rarely let anyone see. But today, it was different. Today, the sadness seemed to wrap around him like a suffocating cloak, and she couldn't bear to stand idly by.

She reached out, her hand hovering for a moment, unsure if he would accept her touch. Then, as if some invisible barrier had shattered between them, she gently wrapped her arms around him. Ahaan stiffened for a brief second, unused to such tenderness. But Aliza's warmth was undeniable, and slowly, almost imperceptibly, he relaxed into her embrace. His breath hitched; a sound so quiet she might have missed it if she wasn't holding him so close. It was the first hug he had ever received, and the realization hit him like a tidal wave. He hadn't known how much he needed this, how much he had longed for this simple human connection. But as he felt her warmth enveloping him, a sense of peace washed over him. It was a hug unlike any he had ever experienced. There was no awkwardness, no hesitation. It was simply a connection, a moment of pure understanding.

Aliza's arms tightened around him, her chin resting lightly on his shoulder. She didn't speak, and neither did he. Words weren't needed in that moment. There was something pure in the silence between them, something sacred about the way they fit together—like two puzzle pieces finally finding their place.

Ahaan's heartbeat was loud in his ears, each pulse a reminder that he was still here, still alive, and that someone cared enough to hold him when the world felt too heavy. Aliza's scent—lavender and something faintly sweet—filled his senses, grounding him, pulling him back from the edge of the abyss he had been teetering on.

For Aliza, the moment was as overwhelming as it was gentle. She had always known there was something different about Ahaan, something fragile beneath the stoic exterior he wore. But feeling him in her arms, feeling the way he slowly surrendered to the comfort she offered—it was as if she could feel the weight of his pain, and in return, she gave him her strength.

Her fingers lightly brushed the nape of his neck, a small gesture, but it sent a shiver through him. Ahaan's hand found hers, hesitant but steady, and he held onto it as if it were the only thing keeping him anchored in that moment.

Their breathing synced, slow and steady, as if their souls were whispering to each other in a language neither had ever spoken before. It wasn't a grand declaration of love, but something far deeper—a quiet understanding, a connection that transcended words.

In that embrace, time seemed to stop. For the first time, Ahaan didn't feel the crushing weight of his past or the uncertainty of his future. All that mattered was Aliza, holding him like he was something precious, something worth saving.

And for Aliza, in that moment, she knew that her heart had found its home in him.

Aliza whispered in his years – "Don't worry, I am always with you, in you, in your heart".

Ahaan pulled her closer, his arms instinctively wrapping around her and whispered back – "I love to love you".

He had never been such close to a girl, he had never been loved so much.

Ahaan thanked her for her understanding and support. As they were about to part ways, he handed her a letter. "Read this when I'm not around," he said. "These are my feelings for you. And one more thing—don't expect it to rhyme."

With a final exchange of smiles, they left the café.

Aliza read the letter on her way home – which read -

In the quiet of the night, I think of you,
Of all the things I wish I could say.
But words escape me, like shadows in the dark,
And I'm left with only silence and the ache in my heart.
I want to tell you everything, to bare my soul,
But fear holds me back, a chain I can't break.
You are the light in my life, the warmth in my cold,
Yet I am lost in a storm, unable to find my way.
I see you, Aliza, the love in your eyes,
And it breaks me to know that I am hiding from you.
But this fear, this shadow from my past,
It's a part of me that I don't know how to fight.
I am scared, Aliza, of what you'll see,
If you look too closely at the man I try to be.
But I love you, more than words can express,
And I pray that one day, I'll have the strength to confess.
For now, I can only hope that you'll stay,
That you'll see the man beneath the fear and the pain.
Because without you, Aliza, I am lost,
A soul adrift in a sea of memories and ghosts.

Tears of happiness glistened in her eyes as she treasured the letter in her bag.

14 - Something Is Cooking

Aliza pushed open the door to her shared room with a growing sense of unease. The room was eerily quiet, devoid of Nadeem's usual presence. She looked around, noting the unmade bed and the cluttered desk, but no sign of him. The room felt strangely empty, as if something was missing.

A deep sense of worry gnawed at her. Nadeem had been acting strangely lately and Ahaan's revelation about the diary only added to her concerns. Without wasting another moment, she grabbed her phone and dialed Nadeem's number.

The phone rang for what felt like an eternity before Nadeem finally picked up. "Hello?" His voice was muffled, as if he were in a noisy place.

"Nadeem, where are you?" Aliza's voice was sharper than she intended, a mix of worry and frustration seeping through. "I came back to the room, and you're not here."

"I'm at the cybercafé," Nadeem replied, his tone casual, almost too casual. The sound of clicking keys and distant voices filtered through the line.

"What are you doing there?" Aliza asked, trying to keep her voice steady despite the rising anxiety within her. "You've been spending so much time there lately, and now Ahaan's diary is missing. Do you know anything about that?"

There was a brief pause on the other end of the line before Nadeem responded, "I'm just handling some stuff, nothing major. Don't worry about it, Aliza."

Aliza frowned, her suspicion growing. "Nadeem, this isn't like you. You're always upfront with me, but now you're being secretive. What's going on?"

"I told you, it's nothing," Nadeem insisted, his voice carrying a hint of irritation now. "I'm just taking care of some personal matters. I'll be back soon, okay?"

Aliza sighed, sensing that she wasn't going to get any more information out of him over the phone. "Fine, but we need to talk when you get back. There's something I need to ask you."

"Sure, whatever," Nadeem muttered before abruptly ending the call.

Aliza stared at her phone, feeling a knot tighten in her stomach. Something was definitely off, and Nadeem's evasiveness only heightened her concern. She tried to shake off the uneasy feeling, but it clung to her like a shadow.

As she sat on the edge of her bed, her phone rang again, startling her. The number on the screen belonged to her publisher. With a deep breath, she answered the call, hoping for some distraction from the unsettling thoughts about Nadeem.

"Hello?" Aliza greeted, trying to keep her voice steady.

"Aliza! I'm glad I caught you," the publisher's cheerful voice boomed through the phone. "I've got some exciting news for you."

Aliza forced a smile, though the worry still lingered in the back of her mind. "Oh? What's the news?"

"We're moving forward with the publication of that poetry book," the publisher announced, his enthusiasm palpable. "You never told me you had such a talented friend!"

Aliza blinked, taken aback. "A talented friend? What do you mean?"

"Don't be modest," the publisher chuckled. "We've been reviewing the manuscript that Nadeem sent over. The poems are brilliant, absolutely captivating. We're planning a major release, and we just need the account details to send the advance royalty to Mr. Ahaan. You know, the author."

Aliza's heart skipped a beat. "Wait, what? Ahaan's poems? Nadeem sent you Ahaan's poems?"

"Exactly," the publisher confirmed, still oblivious to Aliza's growing shock. "Nadeem said Ahaan was a bit shy about submitting his work, but we're thrilled to be publishing such raw, emotional poetry. It's going to be a super duper hit!"

Aliza's mind raced, trying to process the information. The missing diary, Nadeem's strange behavior, and now this—everything was starting to connect. "I... I didn't know," she stammered, her thoughts swirling in confusion. "When did you receive the manuscript?"

"Just a few days ago," the publisher replied. "Nadeem was very professional about it; said he was acting on behalf of Ahaan. We've already started the process, so we just need those account details. Could you ask Ahaan to send them over?"

"I... I'll talk to him," Aliza managed to say, her voice barely above a whisper. "Thank you for letting me know."

"Of course! And congratulations to your friend. We're all looking forward to the release."

Aliza ended the call and sat in stunned silence. The pieces were falling into place, but the picture they formed was one she never expected. Nadeem had taken Ahaan's diary—his private, deeply personal collection of poems—and submitted it to a publisher without Ahaan's knowledge or consent. It was an act that, while seemingly well-intentioned, felt like a betrayal.

Her mind buzzed with questions. Why had Nadeem done this? What had driven him to take such a drastic step? And how would Ahaan react when he found out?

Unable to sit still any longer, Aliza stood up and began pacing the room, her thoughts a chaotic whirlwind. Nadeem was her brother, someone she trusted, but this... this was something else entirely. She needed answers, and she needed them now.

Determined to confront Nadeem, Aliza grabbed her jacket and headed for the door. As she stepped out into the corridor, her phone buzzed with a text message. She paused and glanced at the screen, hoping it was Nadeem with some explanation. But it was just another notification from the publisher, this time asking for a headshot of Ahaan to accompany the book's promotion.

The request felt surreal, like a bizarre twist in a story she didn't understand. She couldn't shake the feeling that this was all spiraling out of control, that something fundamental had shifted in her relationships with both Ahaan and Nadeem.

With her heart pounding, Aliza made her way to the cybercafé where Nadeem had said he was. The streets were busy with the evening rush, but Aliza barely noticed the world around her, her mind too preoccupied with the looming confrontation.

When she finally reached the cybercafé, she hesitated outside the door, taking a deep breath to steady herself. She had no idea what she was going to say, how she was going to approach this, but she knew she couldn't delay any longer.

Pushing the door open, Aliza stepped inside. The café was dimly lit, with rows of computer screens casting a pale glow over the faces of the people engrossed in their work. The faint hum of electronics filled the air, punctuated by the occasional click of a mouse or the tap of a keyboard.

It didn't take long to spot Nadeem. He was seated at a corner terminal, his back to the door, completely absorbed in whatever he was doing on the screen. Aliza approached him slowly, her footsteps barely making a sound on the tiled floor.

"Nadeem," she called softly, trying to keep her voice calm.

Nadeem jumped slightly, clearly startled. He quickly minimized whatever was on the screen before turning to face her. "Aliza, what are you doing here?"

"I need to talk to you," Aliza said, her tone firmer now. "It's important."

Nadeem frowned; his expression guarded. "What's going on? Why do you look so serious?"

Aliza took a deep breath, choosing her words carefully. "I just got a call from my publisher. They said they received a manuscript from you—a book of poems written by Ahaan."

Nadeem's eyes flickered with something—guilt, maybe—but he quickly masked it. "Yeah, I thought it was time Ahaan's work got recognized. He's been sitting on those poems for too long, and they're too good to just keep hidden away."

Aliza's heart sank. "Nadeem, you can't just do something like that without his permission. Those poems are deeply personal to him. He wasn't ready for this."

Nadeem's jaw tightened, and he crossed his arms defensively. "I was trying to help him, Aliza. He's always been so hesitant, so afraid to put himself out there. I thought this could be a good thing for him."

"But did you ask him?" Aliza pressed, her voice trembling with emotion. "Did you even consider how he might feel about this?"

Nadeem looked away, his expression hardening. "I know Ahaan. He would never have agreed to it, no matter how much he needs it. Sometimes you have to push people to take that first step."

Aliza shook her head, disbelief washing over her. "Nadeem, this isn't just about pushing someone. It's about respect, about trust. You've taken something that belongs to Ahaan, something he wasn't ready to share, and made a decision for him. That's not your place."

Nadeem stood up abruptly, frustration etched on his face. "I was trying to do the right thing! Ahaan's been drowning in his own fears, and I thought this could be a way out for him. Why can't you see that?"

"Because you didn't give him a choice!" Aliza shot back, her voice rising. "You took away his agency, his right to decide when and how to share his work. And now he's going to find out from a publisher, not from you, not from a friend he trusts."

Nadeem's face fell, and for a moment, he looked lost, as if realizing the gravity of what he'd done. "I... I didn't mean for it to go this way. I just wanted to help."

Aliza softened slightly, seeing the conflict in his eyes. "I know you did, Nadeem. But you have to understand that this wasn't your decision to make. You've crossed a line, and now we have to figure out how to fix this."

Nadeem slumped back into his chair, rubbing his forehead as if trying to stave off a headache. "What do we do now?"

Aliza thought for a moment, her mind racing. "We have to tell Ahaan the truth. He deserves to know what's happened before he hears it from anyone else. And then... we'll deal with the fallout together."

Nadeem nodded slowly, his bravado fading. "You're right. I'll tell him... I'll explain everything."

Aliza gave him a small, reassuring smile. "We'll do it together. But first, let's get out of here. We need to find Ahaan and talk to him."

As they left the cybercafé, Aliza couldn't shake the feeling that this was just the beginning of a difficult conversation, one that would test the bonds of friendship and trust. But she knew they had to face it head-on, for Ahaan's sake and for the sake of their own relationships.

The walk back to their apartment was tense, the air thick with unspoken words. Aliza could feel the weight of what was to come pressing down on her, but she steeled herself, determined to be there for Ahaan in whatever way he needed.

When they finally reached the guesthouse where Ahaan was living right now, they found Ahaan startled to see both of them at the door.

"Hey, what's going on?" Ahaan asked, sensing the tension between them.

Aliza and Nadeem exchanged a glance before Nadeem stepped forward, his hands trembling slightly. "Ahaan, there's something I need to tell you. Something important."

Ahaan's brow furrowed in concern. "What is it?"

Nadeem took a deep breath, his voice shaky. "I... I took your diary. The one with all your poems. And I sent it to a publisher."

For a moment, there was silence. Ahaan stared at Nadeem; his expression unreadable as the words sank in. Then, slowly, the color drained from his face.

"You did what?" Ahaan's voice was barely above a whisper, filled with disbelief.

Nadeem swallowed hard, unable to meet Ahaan's gaze. "I thought... I thought it was time for your work to be recognized. I didn't want to see you hide away something so beautiful. I'm sorry, Ahaan, I really am. I didn't mean to hurt you."

Ahaan stood up, his body tense with shock and anger. "You had no right, Nadeem. Those poems are personal. They're a part of me that I wasn't ready to share. How could you just take that decision out of my hands?"

Nadeem winced at the harshness in Ahaan's voice, but he didn't back down. "I know I was wrong. I see that now. But I did it because I care about you, because I believe in your talent. I just wanted to help."

Ahaan shook his head, the anger giving way to a deep, aching hurt. "But you didn't ask me. You took something that belongs to me and made it public without my consent. Do you have any idea what that feels like?"

Nadeem finally looked up; his eyes filled with regret. "I'm sorry, Ahaan. I really am. If I could take it back, I would. But now we have to figure out how to move forward."

Ahaan clenched his fists, his mind a whirlwind of emotions. He wanted to lash out, to yell at Nadeem for the betrayal, but he also knew that his friend had acted out of misguided love and concern. It didn't make it right, but it made it harder to hate him for it.

Nadeem was on the verge of crying. He was just a teenage boy, not yet fully equipped to handle such strong emotions. The weight of the situation was pressing down on him, and he looked more like a child who had been caught in a mistake than someone who had intentionally caused harm.

Aliza stood to the side, her eyes darting between the two friends, trying to figure out the right words to say. The tension in the room was thick, and she felt as if she were on the edge of a precipice, unsure of how to pull them back to solid ground.

In the midst of this strained silence, Ahaan suddenly broke the tension with an unexpected question, "How much are they paying as advance royalty?"

Both Aliza and Nadeem looked at Ahaan, completely taken aback. The shock was clear on their faces, and for a brief moment, no one said anything. Then, slowly, a smile crept onto Ahaan's face, followed by a chuckle. "Just look at your faces," he said, laughing outright.

Nadeem, caught between relief and lingering guilt, couldn't help but join in. His laughter was a mixture of nervousness and pent-up emotion. He reached out and punched Ahaan lightly on the arm, the action more playful than anything else. "You jerk," he said, his voice trembling as tears welled up in his eyes.

Ahaan's laughter softened as he watched Nadeem, realizing just how much the whole situation had affected his friend. Without thinking, he pulled Nadeem into a rough hug, the two of them tumbling onto the bed together. Nadeem finally let the tears fall, crying not just out of guilt, but also out of the relief that Ahaan wasn't pushing him away.

Aliza stood there, watching the two of them, a smile forming on her lips. The sight of their bond, so raw and real, warmed her heart. For a moment, the tension was forgotten, replaced by a sense of comradeship that only deep friendships could bring.

As the laughter and tears subsided, Ahaan finally sat up, wiping his eyes. He looked at Nadeem, his expression turning serious again. "But listen, before the book comes out, I need to take down a few of the poems. They're too personal, not meant for anyone but me."

Nadeem nodded; his face still flushed from crying. "Of course. Whatever you want. Just tell me which ones."

Ahaan smirked, his tone lightening as he teased, "Now you're talking like a professional literary agent. Who knew my best friend would turn into my agent overnight?"

Nadeem laughed; the sound more genuine now. "Well, someone's gotta keep you in check."

The three of them sat together, the tension easing as they talked about the next steps. Ahaan's anger had softened into something more manageable, and Nadeem's guilt was starting to lift. Aliza felt a sense of peace settle over her as she watched them, knowing that they had all come out of this stronger.

*****

For the next few days, Ahaan immersed himself in the whirlwind of finalizing the list of poems and diving into promotion activities with the publisher. The process was exhilarating, a stark contrast to the emotional turbulence he'd experienced just a short while ago. He was now navigating the excitement of seeing his work come to life in a way he had never anticipated.

Aliza watched him with a quiet sense of peace, relieved to see the joy that now lit up Ahaan's face. The burden that had once weighed him down seemed lighter, and the smile that had been so rare was now becoming more frequent.

Ahaan was constantly on the move, meeting with the publisher, discussing marketing strategies, and even brainstorming ideas for the book launch. The energy was contagious, and Aliza couldn't help but feel a deep satisfaction in seeing him so engaged and happy.

One evening, after a particularly productive meeting with the publisher, Ahaan returned to their shared space, his face glowing with excitement. "Aliza, I can't believe how far we've come," he said, his voice filled with awe. "This book... it's actually happening. And I couldn't have done it without you and Nadeem."

Aliza smiled, her heart swelling with pride. "We're just happy to see you happy, Ahaan. You've worked so hard for this, and you deserve every bit of it."

Ahaan nodded, his expression softening. "I'm so grateful for everything—your support, your patience. I know it hasn't been easy, but I'm glad we're here now."

As the launch date approached, the anticipation grew. Ahaan was buzzing with ideas and plans, and Aliza found herself swept up in his enthusiasm. It was a beautiful change from the uncertainty and tension that had previously clouded their lives.

Through it all, Ahaan couldn't stop expressing his gratitude to both Aliza and Nadeem. Their friendship, their love had been tested, but it had come out stronger on the other side. And now, as they prepared to share Ahaan's work with the world, there was a sense of accomplishment that bound them even closer together.

As the day of the book launch drew near, Ahaan couldn't help but feel a mixture of nervousness and excitement. This was a moment he had never imagined for himself, yet now that it was here, he was ready to embrace it fully. And with Aliza and Nadeem by his side, he knew he could face whatever came next.

15 - On The Day Of The Book Launch

7:00 AM – Guesthouse where Ahaan stayed

The morning of the book launch had dawned bright and clear, a perfect backdrop for what was supposed to be one of the most important days of Ahaan's life. From the moment he woke up, Ahaan could feel the excitement bubbling inside him. The day he had been working towards, the culmination of all his efforts, was finally here.

But with that excitement came a creeping sense of anxiety. He was restless, pacing around the apartment, checking his phone for messages from the publisher, double-checking the time, and going over the launch day schedule in his head. Everything needed to be perfect.

Aliza had noticed his nervous energy and had tried her best to calm him down. "Everything is going to be fine, Ahaan," she had reassured him over breakfast. "You've done all the hard work, and now it's time to enjoy the moment."

Ahaan had smiled at her, but the worry in his eyes hadn't dissipated. "I just want everything to go smoothly," he had murmured, fiddling with the spoon in his hand. "This is so important."

And so, when the clock struck one in the afternoon and it was time to head to the publisher's office to sign the final formalities, Ahaan felt like he was stepping onto the biggest stage of his life. This was the first time he would be meeting the publisher in person, and he was determined to make a good impression.

"I want you and Nadeem to come with me," he had told Aliza, his voice a mix of excitement and nervousness. "You both have been with me through all of this. I want you there."

Aliza had hesitated, her face clouding over. "I wish I could, Ahaan, but I have some things to take care of before the launch. I'll meet you there directly, okay?"

Ahaan had felt a pang of disappointment but had understood. "Alright," he had said, trying to hide his reluctance. "I'll see you at the launch then."

With that, he had left for the publisher's office.

When he finally arrived at the publisher's office, Ahaan took a deep breath to steady himself. This was it. He was about to meet the person who believed in his work enough to bring it into the world.

The office was sleek and modern, with floor-to-ceiling windows that offered a stunning view of the city. Ahaan was led to a spacious conference room where the publisher, Nadeem, was waiting for him. Fahad was a tall, imposing man with a kind smile, and he greeted Ahaan warmly.

"It's a pleasure to finally meet you, Ahaan," Fahad said, shaking his hand firmly. "We've been very excited about your book."

Ahaan returned the smile, feeling a bit more at ease. "Thank you, sir. I'm honored to be working with you."

As they sat down to discuss the final details, the door to the conference room opened, and Fahad's wife walked in. She was a graceful woman with a gentle demeanor, her belly swollen with the unmistakable curve of late pregnancy. She smiled warmly at Ahaan as she took a seat beside her husband.

But the moment Ahaan's eyes fell on her, something inside him snapped. His heart started to race, his breath coming in short, shallow gasps. The familiar, suffocating feeling of panic washed over him, and before he could stop himself, he was on his feet, the chair scraping loudly against the floor.

"I—I'm sorry, I need to go," he stammered, his voice barely above a whisper.

Fahad looked at him in confusion. "Ahaan, is everything alright?"

But Ahaan didn't answer. He bolted out of the room, the walls closing in on him as he ran down the hallway, ignoring the concerned voices calling after him. He burst out of the building, the cool afternoon air hitting his face like a slap, but it did nothing to calm the storm raging inside him.

He didn't stop running until he was far away from the office, his legs finally giving out as he collapsed onto a bench in a small park. He was shaking, his mind a whirl of confusion and fear. The image of Fahad's wife, her pregnant belly, was seared into his mind, bringing back memories he had tried so hard to bury.

Why now? he thought desperately. *Why does this have to happen now, of all times?*

For hours, Ahaan sat there, his thoughts a chaotic mess. He knew he should call Aliza, explain what had happened, but the thought of hearing her voice, of telling her about his breakdown, was too much to bear. Instead, he shut his phone off, shutting out the world as he tried to wrestle with the emotions tearing him apart.

5:00 PM – The Venue of the Book Launch

As the sun began to set, casting long shadows over the city, the venue for Ahaan's book launch was abuzz with activity. The stage was set, the lights were being adjusted, and the room was filled with the hum of anticipation. Everything was ready—except for one crucial element.

Ahaan was nowhere to be found.

Aliza stood near the entrance, her phone pressed to her ear, her face etched with worry as the call went to voicemail yet again. "Come on, Ahaan, pick up," she muttered under her breath, glancing around the room as if he might appear out of thin air.

Nadeem, who had been pacing back and forth, his own nerves fraying, came over to her. "Any luck?" he asked, though he already knew the answer.

Aliza shook her head, her frustration and fear mounting. "He's not answering. I don't know where he is, and we're running out of time. The guests are going to start arriving soon, and the publisher is already here."

Nadeem ran a hand through his hair, his mind racing. "This isn't like Ahaan. He wouldn't just disappear like this, not today of all days."

Aliza nodded, her mind whirling with possibilities. Where could he have gone? Why would he just leave like that? She thought back to their last conversation, trying to remember if there had been any signs of distress that she had missed.

The sound of footsteps interrupted her thoughts, and she turned to see Fahad walking towards them, his expression a mix of concern and impatience.

"Aliza, Nadeem," he greeted them with a tight smile. "I don't mean to pressure you, but we're running behind schedule. Have you heard from Ahaan?"

Aliza forced a smile, trying to mask her anxiety. "Not yet. He should be here soon."

Fahad nodded, though his eyes betrayed his worry. "I hope so. We have a lot riding on this launch. Please, keep me updated."

As he walked away, Aliza felt a pang of guilt. She knew the publisher had put a lot of faith in Ahaan's work, and the thought of letting him down was almost too much to bear. She turned back to Nadeem, her voice barely above a whisper. "We have to find him. We can't let this fall apart."

Nadeem nodded, his own resolve hardening. "I'll check with some of his friends, see if anyone has seen him. You keep trying his phone."

As Nadeem hurried off, Aliza took a deep breath and redialed Ahaan's number, her heart pounding with every unanswered ring. She couldn't shake the feeling that something was terribly wrong, but she had no idea what to do about it.

The minutes ticked by, each one feeling like an eternity. The room was slowly filling up with guests, all of them chatting excitedly, oblivious to the panic brewing behind the scenes. Aliza could feel the weight of their expectations pressing down on her, and for the first time, she wondered if they would be able to pull this off.

And then, just as she was about to call Nadeem back, her phone buzzed in her hand. The screen lit up with Ahaan's name, and she answered it so quickly that she almost dropped the phone.

"Ahaan! Where are you?" she demanded, her voice a mix of relief and frustration.

There was a pause on the other end, and when Ahaan finally spoke, his voice was low and shaky. "I'm sorry, Aliza. I—something happened, and I couldn't... I just couldn't."

Aliza's heart sank. "Ahaan, what are you talking about? Where are you?"

"I don't know," he admitted, his voice barely audible. "I'm in a park somewhere. I just needed to get away."

Aliza closed her eyes, fighting back the tears that threatened to spill over. "Ahaan, you need to come back. The launch is in an hour. Everyone's waiting for you."

"I can't," he whispered, and the raw vulnerability in his voice broke her heart. "I saw the publisher's wife... she's pregnant, Aliza. I couldn't handle it. I just... I lost it. I am not the person who could come out and face the world."

Aliza felt a wave of understanding. Of course. She had been so focused on the logistics of the day that she hadn't considered how something like that might affect Ahaan. But now wasn't the time for explanations or apologies. Now, she needed to get him back.

"Ahaan, listen to me," she said, her voice firm but gentle. "I know this is hard, but you've come too far to give up now. This is your night. You can't let this moment slip away because of something that happened in the past."

There was a long silence on the other end, and Aliza could almost hear the wheels turning in Ahaan's mind as he weighed her words.

Finally, he sighed. "You're right. But… But… I just… I am sorry. I am coming."

Aliza felt frustrated, but she kept her tone steady. "Don't apologize. Just get here as soon as you can. We'll handle everything else."

As she hung up the phone, Aliza let out a shaky breath. She didn't have time to process everything that had just happened, but at least now there was hope. Ahaan was on his way, and with any luck, they would be able to salvage the evening.

She quickly found Nadeem and told him the news. "He's coming back. He had a bit of a meltdown, but he'll be here soon."

Nadeem's shoulders sagged with relief. "Thank God. I was starting to think we'd have to cancel the whole thing."

Aliza shook her head, determination flashing in her eyes. "We're not canceling anything. This is Ahaan's night, and we're going to make sure it's everything he dreamed it would be."

6:30 PM

The minutes seemed to drag on as the clock inched closer to seven. The guests had all arrived, the room buzzing with anticipation. Aliza and Nadeem hovered near the entrance, their eyes constantly darting to the door, waiting for any sign of Ahaan.

Fahad approached them again, his expression tense. "We need to start soon. The guests are getting restless."

Aliza nodded, trying to hide her own anxiety. "He'll be here. Just a few more minutes."

Just then, the door swung open, and Ahaan stepped into the room. He was disheveled, his hair tousled and his clothes slightly rumpled, but he was here. He met Aliza's eyes across the room, and she could see the apology written all over his face.

Without wasting a moment, Aliza and Nadeem rushed over to him. "Thank God you're here," Aliza whispered, her voice filled with relief. "Are you okay?"

Fahad's impatience was palpable as he rushed over to Ahaan, his hand gripping Ahaan's shoulder. "We need to go to the stage now. We'll handle the formalities later," he urged, his voice tight with urgency.

But before they could move, Aliza stepped forward, her eyes locked on Ahaan. "I need a few minutes with him," she said, her tone leaving no room for argument.

Fahad's frustration boiled over. "Aliza, we're already running late. The guests—"

"Trust me," she interrupted, her voice steady. "These few minutes are necessary."

Fahad looked at her, torn between the pressure of the event and the conviction in her voice. After a tense moment, he sighed and stepped back, gesturing for them to go. Aliza took Ahaan's hand, leading him down a quiet corridor to a small room tucked away in the corner of the venue.

As they reached the door, Aliza paused, her grip on Ahaan's hand tightening slightly. "There's someone here you need to see," she said softly, her eyes searching his.

Ahaan's brow furrowed in confusion, but before he could ask, Aliza gently pushed open the door and stepped aside. Inside the room, standing by the window with her back to them, was a woman. Her shoulders were hunched slightly, as if she carried the weight of years of regret and sorrow. When she turned around, Ahaan's breath caught in his throat.

It was his mother.

For a moment, the world seemed to stop. Ahaan's heart pounded in his chest, a storm of emotions swirling inside him—shock, anger, hurt, and something deeper, something he hadn't allowed himself to feel for a long time.

"Mom…" The word slipped out, barely a whisper, as he took a hesitant step forward.

His mother's eyes filled with tears as she took in the sight of her son, a son she hadn't seen in years. "Ahaan," she breathed, her voice trembling with emotion.

Aliza, sensing the intensity of the moment, quietly slipped out of the room, leaving the two of them alone. The door clicked shut behind her, and Ahaan found himself standing there, face-to-face with the woman who had shaped so much of his life, for better or worse.

For a long moment, neither of them spoke. The silence between them was heavy, laden with years of unspoken words and unresolved pain. Ahaan's mind raced, torn between the anger that had simmered inside him for so long and the overwhelming sense of longing that seeing his mother stirred in him.

"You're angry," she finally said, her voice soft and filled with regret. It wasn't a question; it was a statement of fact, one that she had known all along.

Ahaan clenched his fists, his jaw tightening. "I was a kid, Mom. I didn't understand what was happening, and you... you made me feel like I was the problem." His voice was low, controlled, but there was an edge to it, a sharpness born of years of buried pain.

His mother's face crumpled, the tears she had been holding back finally spilling over. "I was wrong, Ahaan. I was so wrong. I was overwhelmed, scared, and I took it out on you. I've regretted it every single day since."

Ahaan's anger flared again, hot and fierce. "You weren't there for me, Mom. You were supposed to protect me, but instead, you made me afraid—afraid of you, afraid of everything."

She nodded, her tears flowing freely now. "I know. I failed you in the worst possible way. And I'm so, so sorry. I don't expect you to forgive me, but I need you to know that I never stopped loving you, not for a single moment."

Ahaan felt the tears welling up in his own eyes, but he fought them back, his emotions a chaotic mix of anger, sorrow, and longing. "Why now? Why are you here now, after all these years?"

She took a step closer, her hands trembling as she reached out to him. "Because I couldn't stay away any longer. I've watched you from afar, seen how much you've grown, how much you've accomplished. But I know there's a part of you that's still hurting, and I needed to be here, to tell you that I'm proud of you, that I'm sorry, and that I love you."

Ahaan's resolve wavered as he looked into his mother's eyes, seeing the depth of her regret, the sincerity of her words. The anger that had sustained him for so long was beginning to melt away, replaced by an overwhelming sense of grief for the years they had lost.

He took a deep breath, his voice shaky as he spoke. "I spent so many years hating you for what you did, for how you made me feel. But deep down, all I ever wanted was for you to hold me and tell me it was going to be okay."

Her sobs broke the silence, raw and unfiltered, as she finally closed the distance between them and wrapped her arms around him. "I'm so sorry, Ahaan," she whispered through her tears. "I'm so, so sorry."

Ahaan stood there, stiff and uncertain at first, but then slowly, hesitantly, he cradled her in his arms. The anger that had been his constant companion for so long began to dissolve, replaced by a profound sense of release. The walls he had built around his heart were crumbling, and in their place was a tentative hope—a hope that maybe, just maybe, they could start to heal.

They stayed like that for what felt like an eternity, mother and son holding each other as years of pain and misunderstanding finally began to give way to forgiveness. Ahaan knew that it wouldn't be easy, that there was still so much left to confront, but for the first time in a long time, he felt like he could breathe again.

When they finally pulled apart, Ahaan looked at his mother, seeing her not just as the source of his pain, but as a person—flawed, broken, but trying. "I don't know if I can forgive you completely, not yet," he admitted, his voice raw with emotion. "But I want to try. I want to find a way to move forward."

She nodded, wiping her tears with the back of her hand. "That's all I can ask for, Ahaan. I'll be here, for as long as it takes."

There was a knock on the door, and Aliza peeked in, her eyes filled with concern. "It's time," she said gently.

Ahaan looked back at his mother; the weight of the moment still heavy in the air. "Will you stay for the launch?" he asked, his voice softer now.

She smiled through her tears, nodding. "Of course, I wouldn't miss it for the world."

Ahaan turned to Aliza, gratitude filling his heart. She had given him the chance to face his past, to start healing in a way he hadn't thought possible. He reached out and took her hand, squeezing it gently. "Thank you," he whispered.

Aliza smiled, her eyes shining with unshed tears. "You're welcome."

Together, they walked out of the room, ready to face whatever the future held—together, as a family.

16 - Epilogue

The evening cast a golden glow over the venue as the guests began to settle in their seats. The excitement in the air was palpable, a mix of anticipation and curiosity as everyone waited for the event to begin. The stage was set, with a long table at the front where Ahaan, Aliza, Fahad, and a few other key figures from the HJ publishing house would sit. Ahaan's name was prominently displayed behind the stage, along with the title of his book, "Verses of Ahaan's Scars." It was a moment that Ahaan had dreamed of, but never quite imagined it would happen like this.

As the seats filled, Aliza stood off to the side, her hands nervously fidgeting with the hem of her dress. She had always been comfortable in her own space, writing in the quiet solitude of her thoughts, but being in the spotlight was something entirely different. She had initially refused to sit on the stage, preferring to blend into the crowd, but Ahaan and Fahad had other plans.

"Ahaan, I really don't need to be up there," Aliza had protested earlier.

"Nonsense," Ahaan had replied, his tone gentle but firm. "You've been with me through all of this, Aliza. You belong on that stage just as much as I do."

Fahad had chimed in, his usual good-natured grin on his face. "He's right, you know. Besides, the audience would love to see the inspiration behind the man of the hour."

Aliza had blushed at that, her protests falling silent under their combined insistence. And now, as she watched the last of the guests take their seats, she felt a flutter of nerves and excitement.

The lights dimmed slightly, signaling the beginning of the event. Fahad took the stage first, his presence commanding yet warm.

He welcomed everyone with a broad smile, his voice resonating through the room as he spoke about the journey that had led to this moment.

"Ladies and gentlemen, thank you all for being here tonight. It's not every day that we get to witness the birth of something as beautiful as this book," Fahad began, gesturing towards Ahaan. "This evening is special, not just because of the book we're about to launch, but because of the incredible person who wrote it. Ahaan has poured his heart and soul into these pages, and I'm honored to have been a part of bringing it to the world."

The audience responded with applause, and Ahaan felt a warmth spread through his chest. He glanced over at Aliza, who gave him an encouraging smile. It was her silent support that had given him the strength to put himself out there, and for that, he was eternally grateful.

Fahad continued, "But before we dive into the book itself, I'd like to invite Ahaan and the other guests to join me on stage." He gestured towards Ahaan, Aliza, and a few others who were integral to the publishing process.

Ahaan rose from his seat and made his way to the stage, his heart pounding with excitement. Aliza followed, albeit a bit more hesitantly. As she approached the stage, Ahaan held out his hand to her, guiding her up the steps. The gesture didn't go unnoticed by the audience, who smiled at the obvious connection between the two.

Once they were all seated, Fahad opened the floor to questions from the audience. Ahaan knew this was a crucial part of the launch, where he would have to engage directly with the readers who were curious about his work.

The first few questions were straightforward, mostly about Ahaan's inspiration for the book, his writing process, and how he chose the themes that he did. Ahaan answered each question thoughtfully, his voice gaining confidence with each response.

"I've always been fascinated by the way emotions can be captured in words," Ahaan explained in response to one question. "This book is an attempt to give voice to feelings that often go unspoken, to explore the quieter, more introspective moments in life."

The audience seemed to appreciate his honesty and vulnerability, nodding along as he spoke. Ahaan had always been good with words, but seeing the impact his thoughts had on others was a new experience, one that filled him with both pride and humility.

Then came a question that was directed not at Ahaan, but at Aliza. A young woman in the audience stood up, her eyes bright with curiosity. "This question is for Aliza," she began, her voice carrying a note of intrigue. "We know that you went to Varanasi for your own book, and now you're here, supporting your friend's book launch. You met Ahaan in Varanasi, right? Is there something more between the two of you that we should know?"

The question hung in the air, causing a ripple of interest to pass through the audience. Aliza felt a blush creep up her cheeks as all eyes turned towards her. She glanced at Ahaan, who gave her a reassuring nod, his own smile betraying a hint of amusement.

Taking a deep breath, Aliza composed herself and then smiled at the young woman. "That's an interesting question," she began, her voice steady despite the butterflies in her stomach. "My story is still being written, in more ways than one. Maybe this book launch, this very moment, will end up as a chapter in that story. But right now, we're all here to celebrate Ahaan and his incredible work."

"Are you two… I mean… can we expect a love story here?" The counter question came.

"We are…" Aliza looked towards Ahaan. Their eyes met for a moment and then Aliza continued, "We are just friends."

The audience murmured and few laughed as well because the obvious answer to the question was quite visible on the faces of Ahaan and Aliza. Ahaan couldn't help but smile at the way Aliza had gracefully sidestepped the personal nature of the question. Fahad, too, seemed to understand the undercurrent between the two, his own smile widening as he observed them. It wasn't lost on him—or on the audience—that there was something special between Ahaan and Aliza, something that went beyond mere friendship.

Ahaan leaned into the microphone; his voice filled with warmth. "Thank you, Aliza. I couldn't have done any of this without you."

Aliza smiled back, her eyes shining with a mix of emotions. They had been through so much together, and now, as they sat on that stage, it felt like everything had come full circle.

The questions continued, but the atmosphere had shifted slightly. There was a sense of solidarity a shared understanding among those present that this was more than just a book launch—it was a celebration of connections, of relationships that had grown and deepened over time.

As the event neared its end, Fahad took the microphone once more. "Before we conclude, Ahaan has prepared something special for us. He wanted to share a piece of his work that holds a deep personal significance."

Ahaan nodded, standing up to address the audience. His heart raced as he prepared to share something he had kept close to his chest for a long time. "This poem is dedicated to someone who has been my anchor through all of this," he began, his eyes drifting to Aliza. "It's a small token of my gratitude, but it means the world to me."

He paused for a moment, gathering his thoughts before reciting the poem:

In the silence of the night, when the world fades away,
It's your voice that lingers, guiding me through the fray.
You've been my compass, my light in the dark,
In every word, in every smile, you've left your mark.
Through the storms of doubt, through the whispers of fear,
You stood by me, holding my hand, wiping each tear.
I may not say it often, but it's always been true,
In the story of my life, the hero is you.

The room fell silent as Ahaan's voice echoed through the venue, the raw emotion in his words touching everyone present. Aliza felt her heart swell with a mix of emotions—pride, gratitude, and a deep affection for the man standing before her.

As Ahaan finished the poem, he looked directly at Aliza, his eyes reflecting the depth of his feelings. The audience erupted into applause, but for Ahaan, the only person who mattered in that moment was Aliza.

Fahad, ever the observant one, noticed the emotion in the air and decided to wrap things up on that note. "Thank you all for being here tonight," he said, his voice full of warmth. "This has been a truly special evening, and we're so grateful to have shared it with you."

"But before we end this, I also want to thank my literary agent, Mr. Nadeem who did all this for me." Aliza smiled back; her eyes sparkling as usual.

As the guests began to disperse, mingling and discussing the evening's events, Ahaan and Aliza remained on the stage, taking a moment to savor the significance of what had just happened.

"That was beautiful, Ahaan," Aliza said softly, her voice thick with emotion.

"I meant every word," Ahaan replied, his eyes locking with hers. "You've been my strength, Aliza. I wouldn't be here without you."

Aliza's heart fluttered at his words, but before she could respond, Fahad approached them, a knowing smile on his face. "Well, well, I think I just witnessed the beginning of another great story," he teased, his eyes twinkling with mischief.

Aliza blushed, but Ahaan laughed, shaking his head. "Maybe, Fahad. But that's a story for another day."

Fahad nodded, still smiling. "Fair enough. But whatever happens, you two make a great team. I'm looking forward to seeing where this goes."

As the venue began to empty out, Ahaan and Aliza stood together on the stage, watching as the last of the guests filed out. The night had been a success, but more than that, it had marked the beginning of a new chapter in both their lives.

Ahaan turned to Aliza, a soft smile on his face. "Thank you for everything," he said, his voice full of sincerity.

Aliza smiled back with her eyes gleaming as always.

*****

Aliza, who had been standing close to Ahaan, immediately noticed the change in his demeanor. She had seen it before— how his entire body seemed to tense, his eyes flickering with an emotion that she knew was rooted deep in his past. A knot of anxiety began to form in her stomach, and she instinctively reached out, placing a reassuring hand on Ahaan's arm.

But to her surprise, Ahaan didn't pull away. He didn't turn and run as he had earlier in the day. Instead, he stood his ground, his gaze fixed on Fahad's wife as she approached them. Aliza said please don't run away this time and suddenly both of them laughed out loudly. His jaw was set, his posture stiff, but there was something different this time—something resolute in the way he held himself.

Fahad's wife reached them, her face glowing with the joy and anticipation that came with expecting a child. She smiled warmly at Aliza and Ahaan, clearly unaware of the internal struggle that was playing out within him.

"It was such a beautiful event," she said, her voice soft and kind. "Ahaan, your words moved everyone here tonight."

Ahaan nodded, his eyes still locked on her, as if trying to confront the fear that had haunted him for so long. Aliza held her breath, unsure of what to expect. Would he freeze? Would he excuse himself and leave? But Ahaan surprised her once again.

He cleared his throat, his voice a little rough, but steady. "Thank you," he said, his tone sincere. Then, after a brief pause, he said, "I apologize for running away earlier, actually I got reminded of something urgent", both Fahad and his wife replied, "Its ok". Ahaan added - "I'm sure that pregnancy is the most amazing feeling for any woman. Isn't it?"

His words hung in the air for a moment, and Aliza felt a wave of relief wash over her. She glanced at Ahaan, searching his face for any signs of distress, but all she found was a quiet determination—a willingness to face his fear head-on.

Fahad's wife smiled brightly, nodding in agreement. "It truly is. It's a mix of emotions—excitement, joy, a little bit of nervousness—but it's all worth it."

Ahaan nodded slowly, as if absorbing her words. His eyes softened, and for the first time in what felt like an eternity, he looked at a pregnant woman without the shadow of fear darkening his expression. It was a breakthrough, a moment of triumph over the phobia that had gripped him for so long.

Aliza watched this exchange with a mixture of awe and pride. She had known about Ahaan's struggles, had seen firsthand how much it had affected him, but this—this was different. This was Ahaan taking control, refusing to let his past dictate his present.

As the conversation continued, Ahaan's gaze drifted past Fahad's wife, and in the dimming light of the venue, he saw her—his mother, standing near the back of the room. She had stayed out of the spotlight, quietly observing the event, but now, as Ahaan's eyes met hers, she smiled—a soft, loving smile that spoke of understanding and pride.

Ahaan's breath hitched slightly, and for a moment, he felt a wave of emotion threaten to overwhelm him. His mother had been a source of both comfort and pain throughout his life, and yet, here she was, smiling at him with a look that told him she saw the change in him, recognized the growth he had achieved.

Aliza noticed the shift in Ahaan's focus and followed his gaze. When she saw his mother standing there, she knew that this was more than just about overcoming a phobia—it was about healing, about mending the wounds that had festered for so long.

Ahaan turned back to Fahad's wife; his expression now calm, almost peaceful. "I wish you all the best," he said sincerely. "You and Fahad are going to be wonderful parents."

Fahad's wife beamed at the compliment, thanking Ahaan before turning to join her husband, who was wrapping up the last of the evening's formalities.

As she walked away, Ahaan let out a slow breath, as if releasing the last remnants of the fear that had held him captive for so long. He turned to Aliza, who was watching him with an expression of deep affection and respect.

"You did it," Aliza whispered, her voice thick with emotion.

Ahaan gave her a small, almost shy smile. "I guess I did."

In the backdrop, his mother began to make her way towards them, her steps slow and measured, as if she was giving Ahaan time to prepare. But this time, Ahaan didn't feel the need to brace himself. He was ready. Ready to face his past, to confront the pain that had shaped him, and to finally, truly, move forward.

When his mother reached them, there was a moment of silence, a beat where time seemed to stand still. Ahaan looked at her, really looked at her, and saw not just the woman who had caused him pain, but also the woman who had given him life, who had, in her own way, tried to protect him even when it hurt.

"Mom," Ahaan said softly, his voice a blend of old wounds and new understanding.

She reached out, cupping his face in her hands, her eyes glistening with tears. "My son," she whispered. "I'm so proud of you."

Ahaan closed his eyes, leaning into her touch, feeling the warmth of her hands, the love that had always been there, even when it was hard to see. "I'm sorry," he murmured, his voice breaking. "For everything."

His mother shook her head, a tear slipping down her cheek. "No, Ahaan. I'm the one who should be sorry. I didn't know… I didn't understand how much I was hurting you."

Ahaan opened his eyes, meeting her gaze with a newfound clarity.

"We both made mistakes," he said gently. "But I'm ready to move on now. I want to let go of the past."

She nodded, pulling him into a tight embrace. "I'm here for you, Ahaan. Always."

As they stood there, wrapped in each other's arms, Aliza watched them with a soft smile on her face. It was a moment of closure, of healing, and she felt privileged to witness it. Ahaan had not only faced his fears, but he had also taken a step towards rebuilding the relationship with his mother—a relationship that had been strained for so long.

When they finally pulled apart, Ahaan's mother brushed a hand through his hair, just as she had when he was a child. "I'm so happy for you," she said, her voice filled with genuine warmth. "You've come so far, and I know there's so much more ahead of you."

Ahaan smiled at her, his heart lighter than it had been in years. "Thanks, Mom."

She nodded, her eyes still shimmering with unshed tears.

Just then, Ahaan's mom received a call from Rhea. Handing the phone to Ahaan, she said, "It's Rhea." Rhea congratulated Ahaan and thanked Aliza for everything. Ahaan apologized to Rhea, and she readily forgave him. "I'll come see you soon, sis," he promised.

"And Aliza," she added, turning to her, "thank you for being there for my son. I can see how much you care about him."

Aliza blushed slightly but returned the smile. "It's been my honor, really."

With a final smile, Ahaan's mother stepped back, allowing them their space. As she moved away, Ahaan turned to Aliza, his expression full of gratitude.

"I couldn't have done this without you," he admitted, his voice low and sincere.

Aliza shook her head. "You had it in you all along, Ahaan. I just helped you see it."

They stood there for a moment, the evening's events finally catching up with them. The fear, the anxiety, the triumph—all of it settled into a quiet contentment. Ahaan had faced his deepest fears, and in doing so, had found a strength he didn't know he possessed.

As they prepared to leave, Ahaan glanced back at the stage, where only hours earlier, he had been standing in the spotlight, sharing his work with the world. It had been a night of revelations, of growth, and of healing. And as he looked forward, he knew that whatever came next, he was ready to face it head-on, with Aliza by his side.

Hand in hand, they walked out of the venue, leaving behind the echoes of the past and stepping into a future filled with possibilities. Ahaan had won his battle against fear, and now, with his mother's support and Aliza's unwavering love, he felt ready to embrace whatever life had in store for him.

As they reached the outside of the venue, Aliza suddenly stopped, turning to face Ahaan with an intense expression in her eyes. "Ahaan," she began, her voice a mix of seriousness and vulnerability. "I need to say something. I—"

Ahaan's heart skipped a beat, sensing the gravity of the moment. "What is it, Aliza?" he asked softly, his gaze locked on hers.

She took a deep breath, her eyes never leaving his. "I love you,

Ahaan. I've known it for a while, and tonight just made it even clearer. But I have to ask… What happens after marriage? When I get pregnant, are you going to run away?" Her voice wavered slightly, the question filled with both concern and a touch of a playful challenge.

The question hung in the air, and for a brief moment, a serious silence settled between them. Ahaan's mind raced, the weight of her words pressing down on him. But then, as if the tension had burst like a bubble, they both erupted into laughter, the sound echoing through the quiet night.

Ahaan shook his head, his laughter subsiding into a warm, affectionate smile. "Aliza, I think you know by now—I'm done running. I'm here, and I'm not going anywhere."

Aliza's laughter faded into a soft chuckle, and she reached out, taking his hand in hers. "Good," she whispered, her eyes shining with love. "Because I'm not letting you go."

As they stood there, hand in hand, the world around them seemed to fade away, leaving just the two of them in a moment of pure connection. Ahaan knew that this was just the beginning of a new chapter - one that would be filled with challenges, yes, but also with love, laughter, and the promise of a future together.

And as they walked away from the venue, ready to face whatever came next, Ahaan recited the words that had been forming in his heart, a poem that spoke to the journey they had taken together and the one that still lay ahead:

> *In the dance of life, where shadows meet the light,*
> *You've been my partner, guiding me through the night.*
> *With every step, we've faced the unknown,*
> *But with you beside me, I've never been alone.*
> *Through the storms of fear, through the quiet of the dawn,*
> *We've found a rhythm, a beat we can lean on.*

And though the road ahead may twist and bend,
With you, Aliza, I've found my forever friend.
So, here's to the future, to the dreams we'll chase,
To the love we'll nurture, and the fears we'll face.
For in your eyes, I've found my home,
A place where I'm free, a place where I've grown.
The moonlight casts a knowing glance,
On paths untread, a new romance.
In every sigh, in every tear,
A promise blooms, the sequel near.
So, hold me close as this book gently ends,
Knowing soon, a new chapter begins.
And if the world should ever pull us apart,
Know that you'll always have a place in my heart.
For in this life, and the one to come,
You'll be my muse, my love and my only one.

As the final words left his lips, Ahaan looked at Aliza, his heart swelling with a love that was deeper than words could express. She smiled at him, her eyes brimming with unshed tears, and together, they stepped into the night, ready to write the next chapter of their story—a story that was just beginning.

And somewhere in the distance, the promise of another beginning lingered in the air, a future where love would continue to grow, evolve, and thrive, no matter what life had in store.

As the words spilled from him, the weight of his past lifted, like shedding an old, suffocating skin. The secrets he had carried alone for so long now lay between them, raw and vulnerable, and he braced himself for her reaction. But then she stepped forward, tears glistening in her eyes—more than even he had shed—and wrapped her arms around him, holding him so tightly that he could feel her heart beating against his own, as if their souls were intertwining in that very moment. A warmth surged through him, overwhelming in its intensity, and he realized that in her embrace, he had found something sacred—something he hadn't known he was yearning for until now. It was as if the universe itself had granted him its blessings, distilled in the purity of this one embrace. For the first time, he felt truly seen, truly understood, and in her arms, he knew he had found not just love, but a sanctuary where his battered heart could finally rest.

Her tears, however, flowed freely, a silent testament to the depth of her emotions. It was as if a dam had broken, releasing a torrent of pent-up feelings. He had never seen her cry so much before, and it filled him with a sense of both sadness and tenderness. He gently stroked her hair, offering words of comfort and reassurance. In that moment, he knew that their bond was unbreakable, forged in the crucible of shared pain and understanding.

The HAPPY ENDing